THE BLACK BOOK
OF CYRENAICA

Being An Account

of America's Conquest of North Africa in 1805,

With A Description of Several

Troubling Events Experienced on the Campaign,

And an Illustrative Map

a novel by

Bruce McCandless III

ISBN: 0692415726
ISBN 13: 9780692415726
Library of Congress Control Number: 2015905525
Ninth Planet Press, Austin, TX

For Bernice

Many thanks to Pati McCandless, Roger G. Worthington, Jeff Burrus, Jack Wilkinson, Jeff Hunt, Richard Ryan, Jeanette Scott, Pat Cosgrove, Phil West, Edith Wharton, T. E. Lawrence, Shaun Venish, and Chris Beaver.

Illustrations by Chris Beaver.

Map and cover design by Shaun Venish.

CYRENAICA (SY-rə-NAY-ə-Kə): Easternmost portion of the nation once known as Tripoli. Since 2012, Cyrenaica has been a self-declared autonomous region of Libya. It is also the region in which the United States fought its first war on foreign soil.

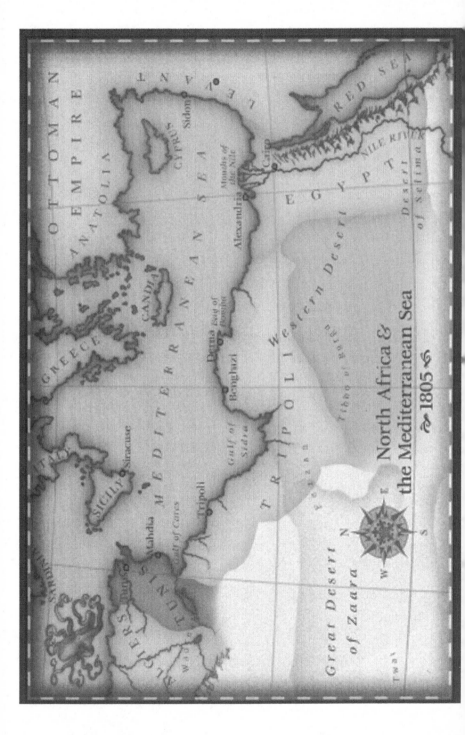

North Africa &
the Mediterranean Sea
1805

Characters

Lemuel Sweet, a private of the U.S. Marines.

Donald MacLeish, also a Marine private, and a native of Baltimore.

Malcolm Weston, leader of the U.S. expedition to place Ahmad Vartoonian on the throne of Tripoli.

Ahmad Vartoonian, rightful ruler of Tripoli, but ousted from his homeland by his younger brother, Yusuf—or "King Yusuf."

Yusuf Vartoonian, usurper of the throne of Tripoli—and younger brother of Ahmad.

Gustav Ladendorf, a man of great learning and facility with languages, a mercenary officer who serves as the expedition's translator.

Daniel Corrigan, a lieutenant of the U.S. Marines, fastidious and valiant.

Ali Rasmin, a favorite of King Yusuf, and appointed by him to be governor of Cyrenaica.

Alfonse Rivera, a Spanish priest and purported emissary from Rome to the Coptic Church of Egypt.

Sheikh al-Tahib, a fierce and imperious desert chieftain, very strict in his faith.

Geoffrey of Bulmershe, a knight of uncommon brutality and zeal who disappeared in the Western Desert in the year 1099, after having helped to conquer Jerusalem.

Prologue

It comes out of the emptiness as it always has and it walks unremarked into the places of men. Though it has many names, none of them are remembered here. It has spent years in the desert. It has slept in shadows and crawled through ancient aqueducts and pulled down, piece by piece, the lonely towers of stone. But the exile is over. The wind brings news. Rumors. Myths. Incitements, in all the broken tongues of the cities. So it mingles with crowds in the streets and alleys and it follows the streamers of sound. This body is failing. It is starting to fray, as so many have before it. The tissue cracks and splits and the liquid grows sticky. The liquid must not escape. The will can hold it. Hold it tight. It is tiresome, this body—as all bodies are. It bends and sags and catches on corners. It cannot move as one wishes. And yet one needs it to work in the world. To reach and touch and pull and tear. So it must be cared for. The thumbs and the feet and the teeth. There are errands to do. To stay strong, it must eat.

1.

First Blood

Behold Yusuf Vartoonian, King of Tripoli. Kin slayer. Consort of witches. The Mediterranean is his bank and larder. From it his pirates take captives, cargo, and some measure of prestige. Yusuf's biggest prize to date is the *U.S.S. Charleston*. The 36-gun frigate runs aground on the Kaliusa Reef, just outside Tripoli's rocky harbor, on December 10, 1804. Captain Josiah Mallory orders the ship's water pumped out. He has several of her cannons thrown overboard and her foremast cut down and jettisoned in order to decrease the vessel's weight, but nothing works. The ship will not budge. She lists fifteen degrees to port, and cannot bring her guns to bear. Surrounded by hostile vessels—xebecs, feluccas, an ancient gallivat—the *Charleston* surrenders without a fight. When the crew refuses an order to strike the flag, a midshipman is sent aloft to do it instead.

King Yusuf's men board the ship half an hour later. They imprison her crew and steal everything they can carry. In the following month they recover the *Charleston's* submerged cannons and tow the captured vessel into port for refitting. America is disgraced.

Nine weeks later, Lieutenant Stephen Decatur sails a lateen-rigged ketch into the harbor under cover of darkness. Decatur seeks redemption for his flag and glory for himself. He sees no clear distinction between the two. He is beautiful and dangerous. Men follow him reflexively. He and his crew board the *Charleston*—now called *Will of the Prophet*—where she stands at anchor. The Americans kill every man they can find. They place barrels of gunpowder in her hold, set the frigate alight, barely manage to escape before the vessel explodes beneath them. It is an incredible feat: the robbers, robbed. The fire in the harbor lights up the city. Dead Moors wash ashore in pieces, a feast for the crabs.

But Yusuf, a bullheaded man who wears a pair of Spanish pistols in his sash, still holds the *Charleston's* three hundred mariners in his prison. Next morning, ten are taken before a mob of Tripolitans and beheaded in their sight. Yusuf vows that the United States will pay dearly for the lives of the rest. If not, the captives will make fine slaves. He will send them to Timbuktoo. There are African potentates who will trade gold for healthy white men, though westerners seldom last long in equatorial climes.

This is the kind of threat that sells newspapers in Philadelphia. Surely the republic didn't kick crazy old King George in the bollocks only to see its citizens enslaved by pagan outlaws. America is outraged. EASTERN BARBARISM—JERUSALEM IN CHAINS—AN AFFRONT TO ALL CHRISTIAN PEOPLES. The Federalists seize the opportunity for political advantage. They say Thomas Jefferson cannot defend the nation from its enemies. The Republicans are weak. The White House must be taken. As a consequence, the embattled President Jefferson will listen to any idea his advisors bring him—even desperate ideas, it turns out. He learns that a mid-level American envoy to Egypt has befriended King Yusuf's brother. The brother, Ahmad by name, has a credible claim to the throne of Tripoli. In return for Jefferson's aid in exercising this claim, Ahmad promises peace and lasting amity with the United States. He says he needs Mexican gold and American muskets. After several days of secret discussions, the President reluctantly approves a plan. Only his closest advisors are allowed to know.

The new nation is going to war.

2.

Americans in Egypt

March 6, 1805

Donald MacLeish takes Lemuel Sweet to the house of the *almee* to see the fabled dancing women. Fable exceeds reality. Three of every four are haggard prostitutes. *Disgusting, obscene creatures,* says MacLeish. *Teeth rotting out of their heads.* But the big man continues to watch, and later he visits the chambers upstairs with no apparent sense of misgiving. Private Sweet declines the offer of sport. There is only one cure for the pox, he knows, and it is almost as painful as the disease itself: One Night with Venus, a Lifetime with Mercury. Instead the young marine sips black coffee in a corner of the salon and attempts to decipher another page of Buffon's massive *Natural History*. The language torments him. He is embarrassed to find himself lingering over the pictures.

Pvt. Lemuel Sweet

MacLeish's return is hushed and hurried. There is the matter of payment. Unhappy with the quality of the services rendered, he has decided to forego this element of the transaction. Noise erupts above them. First comes an anguished female scream, then a series of male responses. MacLeish thinks it advisable to move quickly. Pulling Sweet by one arm, he ducks out the curtained entryway and into the marketplace.

Egypt's oldest city is built on bones: ruin on ruin, corpse hugging corpse. Its streets and alleys twist and fail and turn in upon themselves. This district of Alexandria is a dirty maze, hot and loud and congested. Indeed in the *souk* the crowd is so dense it is hardly possible to approach the tiny raised platforms where merchants sit like unsmiling idols among their wares: olives of a dozen sizes and colors; a soup made of snails; fish still wet from the sea. Turkish soldiers move dark-eyed and distrustful through the eddying masses, staring as if to mark each face. They are briefly astonished by the vagrant Americans, but one look at MacLeish dissuades them from their questions. MacLeish is a massive, long-armed man with formidable eyebrows and a look of perpetual discontent, as if he suspects something is about to be taken from him. He is not afraid to stare back.

Parakeets flit through stripes of sunlight. Fanatics in sheepskins glower from the threshold of a mosque, tufts of wiry hair escaping their faded turbans. A mad African stands gigantically naked against one crumbling wall. His teeth filed to points, his head and face daubed with red pigment, he murmurs Sudanese incantations at the unresponsive crowd. Bare-legged Berber women, tattooed and insolently gay, trade their striped blankets for sugar, tea, and Manchester cotton. From these hundreds of unknown and unknowable people, bound together by cryptic affinities or conspiring against each other with malice covert and untraceable, there emanates an atmosphere of mystery and menace more stifling than the reek of grease and cinnamon and unwashed bodies that hangs like a fog under the patchwork roof.

Lemuel Sweet flinches from the touch of foreign flesh. Blond, slightly built, and mildly nearsighted, he appears to be puzzled by everything he sees. The heat and noise make him dizzy. He is a young man, and much given to whimsy. He thinks that if he listens hard enough, he will understand the dialects around him, and will thereby learn small hidden truths. Although he is not sure he wants to. He is smart enough to recognize the market as the central organ of a native life that extends beyond the city walls into far-off oases and secret clefts of the mountains where plots are hatched and wars of faith and hatred planned—and further still, to the yellow deserts south and west of Alexandria where negroes droop and stumble across the sand as they are driven toward the slave market, that inmost recess of the bazaar where the ancient traffic in muscle and blood proceeds as it always has, enriching pocketbooks but destroying men and women, families and tribes.

It is too much to think about. The men buy a handful of almonds and two cups of tea. It is time to return to camp. At last they walk out from the crowds and chaos of the market and turn their faces west. Privates Lemuel Sweet and Donald MacLeish: U.S. Marines. They stare at the unmarked lanes as if uncertain whether to trust their senses. The sun falls back over the mud-walled houses. It is a patient enemy. Beggars approach, display their afflictions, are brusquely turned away.

"What happened back yonder?" asks the young one. Sweet.

"A den of thieves, son," snaps MacLeish. "That's what happened. And me with my main mast hoisted."

"Again?"

"The world has set its face against me."

"Queer," says Sweet. "How the natives torment you."

"Not hardly. The honest are always abused by the wicked."

They catch the scents of garlic and onions and frying meat, and Sweet grows hungry again. The glassmakers' shops are closing. A child throws stones at them as they pass. Clearly they're lost, but the faces around them are empty of welcome and there seems little chance here of assistance. Sweet's book of natural history grows heavier. Shadows pool in the alleys. In a dirty back lot a woman is adding rocks to a pile and Sweet sees, or imagines he sees, a tiny foot sticking out from the base of the cairn. The marines quicken their pace. But to what end? They have no idea where they're going. When they hear the shouts, it is hard to tell where the sounds are coming from. They stop and cock their heads, straining to identify the source of the commotion. It seems to be getting closer. Only a few yards ahead of them a man in rags bolts from the mouth of an alley. When the hood falls from his head, the marines see fair skin. Two Egyptians spill out of the same alley a few moments later, screaming for blood. The figure they are chasing stumbles, and his pursuers set about beating him with metal-tipped staves. A half-dozen blows rain down upon the figure before the marines realize what they are seeing.

"That's a white man," observes MacLeish.

"Here," Sweet calls. "Leave off! You'll kill him."

Two more Egyptians join the fray. They are unremarkable individuals, garbed in the local attire and possessed of no outward sigil of authority, yet they seem intent on their task. The four of them lay into the fallen westerner. The few people on the street avert their eyes and keep walking. When Sweet takes another step forward, one of the Egyptians whirls and strikes at the young marine. Sweet blocks the blow with his book, but MacLeish has seen enough. He picks up a rock and drops one of the attackers from behind with a sickening crunch of skull. He grabs the arm of another and slams him against the mud bricks of the nearest structure. Now he has a stave. It makes a whooshing sound as he swings it in front of him, carving great slices of air. The Egyptians are appalled. They babble in their native tongue, pointing at the fallen man. MacLeish will have none of it. These Alexandrians are slender creatures, little more than rag and bone. MacLeish often says he could eat one in an afternoon and still have room for pudding. The three who remain upright begin to backpedal. One leaves a sandal in the dust. MacLeish lunges again and this is enough. The assailants break and run.

Sweet helps the injured westerner to his feet. The man blinks the sweat out of his eyes, pauses to blot his mouth with one edge of his robe.

"*Alles*," he says, "*fur ein kleines Madchen.*"

"Are you injured?" asks Sweet.

"Never mind him," says MacLeish, focusing on his companion. "What about you, lad? Nothing broke?"

"I'm fine. The *Natural History* saved me. But I think our friend here took some pretty good blows. Do you speak English, sir? Do you need a doctor?"

The fugitive studies his rescuers. The uniforms. Their faces. Despite the blows he has absorbed, he seems calm. His eyes are a curious shade of yellow.

"Of course," he says. The words come slowly. As if once rehearsed, but now forgotten. The man reaches up to feel his head. He brings back his palm and Sweet is surprised to see it is clean. "A doctor. But where?"

"We have a good one. We're camped out west of the city."

"West? Very well. We shall go."

"Aye. But we're a little turned around."

"*Ach.* Yes. *Verloren.* Then perhaps I shall lead."

One Egyptian remains in the dust, bleeding from his head. MacLeish kicks him as they pass, but the Egyptian doesn't move. The stranger grins. He strolls over to the body, crouches down, and whispers in the man's right ear.

Just as they are about to leave the street, the companions hear a voice behind them. A woman robed in blue and wearing a white veil stands at the site where the skirmish occurred. She points at the stranger between the marines and screams in a language they have never heard before. They understand the sentiment, though. The air is charged with hatred.

The stranger ignores her.

Sweet and his friend exchange shrugs.

"Maybe he didn't pay neither," says MacLeish.

3.

The Liberators

Malcolm Weston has received his orders.

They are not actually signed by the President, of course. Jefferson is too smart for that. Weston has spent many years in politics, and he understands the delicacy of the mission he is about to undertake. The Republicans have long denounced foreign entanglements and the drain on the treasury they entail. Thus, Weston's proposal is not the sort of undertaking the President can be expected to endorse, unless it actually works. But he has received Thomas Jefferson's orders nonetheless, reluctantly relayed by Samuel Barron, admiral of America's Mediterranean fleet. Weston reads the dispatch several times, savoring each word. Admiral Barron is a fussy, unimaginative man who has always been skeptical of Weston's proposals. It must have pained him to send this letter. He has no more marines to spare, he writes—and can by no means dispatch the bomb ketch Weston covets. No matter. The plan is approved. Weston will march his men across the Western Desert and assault the Kingdom of Tripoli's three principal cities—starting with Derna, smallest of the three, moving on to Benghazi, and culminating with the capital, also named Tripoli. He and his army will depose the tyrant Yusuf Vartoonian and replace him with his older brother Ahmad, the rightful heir to the throne. King Yusuf is a menace to commerce. His pirates have stolen cargoes, threatened merchants, and impounded the vessels of a dozen nations, including, most notably, the United States. Prince Ahmad, on the other hand, promises peace—and the immediate release of the crew of the *U.S.S. Charleston.*

Weston's task would be easier if he had transport ships at his disposal, but this is not to be. Awaiting reinforcements to strengthen his blockade of Tangiers, another haven for pirates, Admiral Barron claims his fleet is stretched too thin to shuttle Weston's rabble around the Mediterranean. Besides, the port of Alexandria is closed to Western shipping by order of the Grand Sultan of the Ottoman Empire. Weston therefore proposes to travel overland. He and his coalition of liberators will rally support for Prince Ahmad along the way by means of pamphlet, oratory, and the canny distribution of gifts and trinkets. The expedition will rendezvous at the Bay of Bomba with at least two and possibly an additional ship of the Navy, and Weston will use this opportunity to coordinate the assault on Derna with Captain Isaac Burrus of the *U.S.S. Endeavor*. Derna is the principal port of the eastern province of Tripoli, the land known to the ancients as Cyrenaica. It is hoped that the city will rally to Ahmad's banner and present King Yusuf with a *fait accompli*: loss of the eastern province of his kingdom, along with the prospect of a pincer-movement attack by land and sea against his capital. To be sure, there are practical challenges. Food. Water. Transport. The terrain of the Western Desert itself, which is unequaled in its hostility to human traffic. And yet there is a Point A, and a Point B, and no single insurmountable impediment to transit. Weston sees no choice but to march through the badlands.

The British consul in Alexandria, Sir John Cholmondely, laughs when he hears the plan. He tells Weston he's mad. Says it can't be done.

Weston shrugs. He understands the difficulties. He would like the luxury of options, but there are none at hand. President Jefferson wants him to proceed, and it is his duty as a patriot to obey. He will therefore do what he can. He will cross the desert and capture the city of Derna. He will then move on to Benghazi, and from there launch his assault on the capital city.

He will conquer Tripoli, he tells Sir John. And no one will be laughing then.

* * *

Aside from Weston himself, there are nine Americans in the army the general has assembled to support Prince Ahmad's claim to the throne. The only officer is dark-haired, honey-tongued Lieutenant Patrick Corrigan, a fourth-generation Virginian who has been infected by his commander's manias. Corrigan has a fine aquiline nose and an upper lip that curls in a natural sneer. He leads eight marines on loan from vessels of the Mediterranean fleet. He comes highly recommended. Though slight of stature and reputedly frail, Corrigan has a ferocious devotion to duty. He is here to prove himself. He is desperate for action.

The Americans are joined by a company of twenty-nine Egyptian infantrymen, led by a former Janissary named Selim Comb, and thirty-eight Greek mercenaries under the command of the flamboyantly blasphemous Captain Lako Androutsos. The Greeks are from Thessalonica, members of a local militia who are said to have become too intimate with the bandits they were meant to be policing. Suspected of joining these outlaws in attacks on Turkish officials, the Greeks have been banished from their homeland. Sir John has warned Weston not to use them. The Greeks are dissolute at the best of times, vicious and easily distracted. On the other hand, there is no denying their combat skills. Each is well versed in the arts of ambush and murder, and comes armed with a variety of muskets, pistols, and daggers. Weston waves off Sir John's concerns. The Greeks are welcome, he says—though they charge more than twice the rate of the Egyptians for their services.

Prince Ahmad, the would-be king, has ninety fighting men of varying quality, including those who accompanied him when he fled Tripoli and a dozen mamelukes—Egyptian noblemen—who have sworn allegiance to him since his arrival in Alexandria. There are random recruits besides: rejects and malcontents from the Turkish under-class, skulking Syrian practitioners of the garrote and stiletto, petty thieves from a dozen nations. All in all, this contingent has little to boast about. It is a collection of dreamers and derelicts, cozeners and criminals. It seems ill-equipped to conquer a coffee house, much less a country.

Charged with tending to the health of the expedition is the Italian Jew Alessandro Rizzolo, a self-taught surgeon who wears a maroon felt hat and insists on traveling by camel.

Rizzolo plays poorly at cards and holds dubious theories about the possibility of reanimating the dead through the application of electrical currents. He is often accompanied by the long-haired chevalier Georges LeFebvre, a self-styled nobleman and dangerous duelist whom the British suspect is actually the bastard son of a housemaid to Marie Antoinette. Both men do their best to avoid Alfonse Rivera, a stocky, sad-eyed Spaniard desperately addicted to laudanum and, until engaged in service, the day before the expedition sets out, diligently preparing to die in a gutter.

Sr. Rivera has little to say. He is taken on by Weston because he claims to have visited Benghazi, and thus has knowledge that may come in handy in the course of the expedition. The Spaniard insists that he will not share his quarters, and indeed seems suspicious of everyone he encounters. It is unclear exactly why he wants to march west with the army. Possibly he is like most of the rest of its constituents: he needs the money, and has nothing better to do.

* * *

Also enlisted is the individual recently rescued from a gang of Alexandrian thugs by Privates Lemuel Sweet and Donald MacLeish. This gentleman introduces himself as Gustav Eugene Ladendorf, a Swiss engineer who formerly served as a colonel in his homeland's Tyrol battalions. The Dutchman, as he is called by the marines, who refer to all northern Europeans in this manner, stands five and a half feet tall. He has lion-colored eyes and unusually long fingers. He wears gold-rimmed spectacles, and what little hair he has is reddish-orange. He travels light, with nothing but a leather satchel to his name. Those who have seen it report that it contains only an extra tunic and several green glass jars. He has also requested his own tent, but is otherwise unconcerned by the details of his accommodations. Unlike the Spaniard, he has impeccable manners. Weston is pleased to acquire his services. Ladendorf has knowledge of Mahometan customs. Indeed, he claims to have circumcised himself several years earlier and traveled among the followers of the Prophet as a dervish. To hear him tell it, he has been inside the Holy City, where no infidel is allowed to set foot. He has walked the seven ambits of the Kaaba and kissed the sacred stone that fell from God's hand. Yet he dismisses his former shows of devotion as acts of necessity in a foreign land. He juggles and tells stories. He can make coins appear from thin air. He speaks Arabic, Copt, and a fair amount of Berber, native tongue of the people who formerly ruled these regions. The colonel has a birdlike gaze, curious and unblinking. He says he is eager to help.

* * *

These men, together with a score of Alexandrian cooks and stewards and a number of Bedouin camel drivers and their families, make the whole number of the liberation force about two hundred, along with eighty-four camels, ninety-three goats, twenty-four mules, and sixty-one horses of various breeds and temperaments. This is the force that aims to change the face of North Africa, and assert the will of the fledgling American republic on the world.

* * *

In his camp just west of the city, General Weston bribes and bullies, writes letters, shouts encouragement. He is anxious to set out. The men of the *Charleston*—sailors, naval officers, and a detachment of sixteen marines—languish in underground cells a thousand miles to the west. Their hapless captain writes letters to Admiral Barron containing secret messages scribbled in lime juice. Lieutenant Joseph Wilkerson and four seamen are ill, he reports. Another two have "turned Turk"—converted to Mahometanism—in an attempt to curry favor with their captors. All the men are forced to work fourteen hours a day strengthening the Red Fortress against the threat of American attack. The citizens of Tripoli mock them at their labor; indeed, several of the crew have been injured by thrown stones. At least a dozen have been bastinadoed—suspended upside down and beaten on the soles of the feet until they are unable to walk. As King Yusuf has pledged to burn his prisoners alive if rescue is attempted, American diplomats argue for a measured approach. They implore President Jefferson to refrain from further antagonizing Tripoli.

Malcolm Weston hates talk like this.

"Burnt alive or worked to death," he says. "Either way, our countrymen end up dead. And if our government continues to pay the people's silver to pagans and pirates who threaten our right to engage in lawful commerce, we may as well erase ourselves from the pages of any history of the civilized nations."

Lieutenant Corrigan nods. "Sir," he says. Inside he burns. The invasion of Tripoli will be a mad expedition, completely outnumbered, in a desert that has never been properly mapped. Two hundred against a nation. Thermopylae. The *Anabasis.* Corrigan sees history in his head. It is to be written on parchment, and read by the saints. Surely his name will be mentioned.

✳ ✳ ✳

On the morning of March 10th, this daggle-tail column— marines and Arabs, Greeks and Egyptians, all mixed riotously together—sets out to rescue the crew of the *Charleston* and place Prince Ahmad on the throne of Tripoli. A crowd of farriers and greengrocers, cripples and whores has gathered to see them off. The camels unfold their long legs. Mules shift and stamp as loads are lashed to their backs. Three flags are seen at the head of the column. One is the red and white crescent-moon-and-star of the Ottoman Empire. Another is Ahmad's standard: green, with three white crescents arranged in a pattern that suggests a bull's head and horns. The final flag is the Stars and Stripes—fifteen of each, to honor America's many states.

Two hundred yards to the rear stand Lemuel Sweet and Donald MacLeish, one slight and awkward, the other massively muscled. They laugh at the prospect of personal hazard as only young men can. They have pennies to their name, and no one to wave them goodbye. But the sun is in the east, and they see glory before them. Fortunes can change. They are keen to set off.

"Hard to credit," says MacLeish. "But I think we're finally moving."

"Equally hard to credit," says Sweet. "Our friend from the city. Just there, on the hillside."

"You're having a go."

"I'm quite serious, I assure you."

"Show me."

"See? The one holding the crucifix."

Sure enough, a woman robed in blue, and wearing a white hijab, watches as the army passes. Though her head and most of her face are covered, she seems by size and stature to be the woman who cursed them for rescuing the fallen Colonel Ladendorf two days earlier. MacLeish doffs his hat in mock salute, but the woman has no reaction to the gesture. Her attention is focused instead on the front of the column, almost out of sight by now, where the officers and most of the westerners march. Sweet looks backward a few minutes later. The figure raises her veil and spits on the ground, as if to rid herself of even the tiniest particle of dust or dung that might have come to rest on her lips. Then she steps on the spot where she spat and grinds the dirt beneath her heel. She crosses herself, turns, and begins walking back toward Alexandria.

Indifferent to this bleak send-off, the expedition is under way. The gears of history grind and turn. Another war has begun.

From the Diary of Lemuel Sweet,
March 11, 1805

It is said we are hardly the "pick of the litter," as Mother would put it, insofar as martial reputation is concerned. It is true that not all of the best Marines were desirous of assignment to General Weston, & surely no harsch[1] judgment can attend their reservations in this regard. Cpl. Winters indeed ventured his opinion that we were as Lambs, being led to the Slaughter. And yet at the intersection of ability and interest I think our company is well met. My companions are capable men. The familiar curse of Alcohol walks among us, but this vice is omnipresent in the vessels of a wartime navy, & perhaps will be vanquished here by the extreme difficulty faced in finding a ready supply of the Poison among the Mahometans. Steph. Prejean is called a cripple, due to a deformity in one leg, but is quick to bear a hand and capable of performing any reasonable task. Pvt. O'Dell comes painted as a braggart and a blackguard, but he sings a beautiful tenor. Our gentleman, Lt. Corrigan, lately of Ardent, is sharp but fair. He does not Idle away the hours in-doors, as do some officers, but rather joins us in the elements and offers words of encouragement where warranted.

My mountainous comrade MacLeish is also here of course. His strength is useful on many occasions tho I fear for his Stamina in the miles to come. We are customarily paired in performing the duties of the march and our nightly bivouac, due to our friendship and shared service on the Wasp. Often we discuss the plight of the crew of the Charleston, & the means by which we shall restore our fellow Americans to liberty. MacLeish has a further motivation as well: Plunder. Insofar as

---

[1] Sweet's diary entries are reproduced largely *verbatim*. However, spelling in the 18th and early 19th centuries was irregular at best. Much like the journals of Meriwether Lewis in the American West, which were written at more or less the same time, Sweet's prose contains what to modern eyes look like egregious misspellings of even common words. In order to avoid distraction, Sweet's orthographic and grammatical idiosyncrasies have been "corrected" to reflect 21st Century norms.

it is allowed, and maybe slightly beyond, he intends to sample the ill-gotten riches of Tripoli's tyrant after we have pulled King Yusuf from his throne. This Yusuf is said to be immensely wealthy, due principally to the piratical activities of his subjects. MacLeish believes it would not go amiss if we were to relieve the king of some portion of his treasury. He is a singular specimen, my friend. Gentle in his resting moments, capable even of a rude Philosophy, he is resentful of authority and his social betters. He will, if not checked, argue himself into an apprehension of the World as a place of manifest Injustice and Inequality, and in such humor is susceptible to the slightest insult or affront—particularly when he is in his cups. Once convinced that he has been wronged, he is uncontrollable in his anger. I saw it ship-board on several occasions, & am convinced that he has impeded his own advancement through displays of insubordination brought on by imagined or exaggerated slights. On such occasions I am sometimes called upon to calm the man. I do what little I can. I remind him of his son at home, a lad of tender years, though not of the boy's mother, who is the subject of my friend's darkest rages. I am not always successful. As I have written previously, he was given twenty lashes of the cat o' nine tails in November for the offense of threatening to wrap the bosun's mate around a scupper pump. The lashes cut deep, and one among the wounds grew inflamed, causing my friend great pain and fevers. The rage inspired by that incident has never completely subsided, tho it seems now mostly contained.

At any rate we have started the march. We are determined to assist our American brothers in their time of trial, and to spread the blessings of liberty and representative government to those we meet on our journey west, benighted though they may be!

* * *

I hope it is not impertinent of me to note that alongside my military duties, I am in addition quite hopeful of seeing the fennec fox, a rare species of small dog or wolf (genus Vulpus) that is said to live in this region. Also the varieties of spider and scorpion native to these desert climes, and whatever serpents may present themselves for observation.

4.

Weston

Malcolm J. Weston is talented, inquisitive, and quick to anger. His sideburns are so thick that they suggest buttresses, capable of supporting his head if it were to be removed and consecrated as some boney monument. He is prematurely gray and has a jutting chin, and his shoulders are hunched as if he walked at all times into the wind. He served most notably in Indian country, where he fought the Miamis under Little Turtle in 1792. He holds the redskins in the highest regard, and killed several of them at Fort Reliance. Later he disguised himself and walked among the Shawnees with porcupine quills fixed in his scalp lock. He writes fondly of his former enemies. Their native valor. Truly remarkable. He is a poet of conventional sentiments, an acolyte of George Washington and a student of Alexander the Great's Persian campaigns. He believes fervently in destiny—chiefly his own.

Weston generally dines alone, though he is otherwise gregarious. The general is fastidious about his fingernails. He is said to dislike the fiddle. After dinner in Alexandria he would invite the locals to his tent to listen to Private Hollis Mason's tales of the Indian wars. At the age of sixteen, Mason was present at the Blue Licks with Daniel Boone and the Kentucky militia; indeed, to hear the aging enlisted man tell it, he barely escaped with his scalp. He later witnessed Hugh McGary's murder of the war chief Moluntha with the chief's own hatchet, as the old sachem sat at parlay with General Logan. *Split the redskin's head plumb open*, Private Mason says. *Just like a walnut. You could see his brains.* A disgraceful act, that murder. No gentleman can condone it—and indeed McGary was court-martialed for the deed. Yet the tale serves a purpose. It is good that the Mahometans hear such stories, says Weston. It is useful for them to know that we Americans have dipped our hands in blood. The Arabs of the desert prize physical courage above all other qualities. Courage does not flinch at the prospect of violence. Vengeance is a language the Arabs understand.

The marines reserve judgment about their leader. Malcolm Weston is an officer. This is all they need to know. There is work to do: before dawn, after dark. They are the ones who do it. They are a collection of strong backs and bad attitudes. They are policemen, enforcers, lackeys, brutes. They are highwaymen in government boots, and the men of the Navy despise them as bullies. The marines shrug it off. Sailors are monkeys, leather-skinned creatures of arcane skills and enforced repetition. They are ruled by superstition: omens, curses, ghost ships glimpsed through the fog. It is no great feat to frighten a tar. Most will refuse to set sail on a Friday. They whistle to call the wind. They are handy with knives, and can consume quantities of alcohol that defy belief. But they are better talkers than fighters. It has been proven.

* * *

Weston has shed his civilian attire. The leader of the expedition now wears a uniform of his own devising, featuring a forest green jacket with cream-colored facings and gold epaulets on the shoulders. While he calls himself "general," his authority to do so is unclear, as his most recent military service was twelve years earlier. Since that time he has held a number of positions in state and national government, including Inspector of Hides and Pelts for the State of New Hampshire. Rising with the fortunes of the Republican party, he served as a diplomatic attache to Tangiers, where he feuded with the local emir's foreign minister in spectacular fashion, threatening to horse whip the man if he should meet him on the street. This act led to his banishment from Tangiers, though not from the affections of his political superiors. The threat was widely reported back in the States. The broadsheets loved it. Weston, they said, was a man of backbone. Private Sweet theorizes that Weston has had himself appointed the commander of the makeshift army of Prince Ahmad rather than of any American force. But this only raises more questions. *If Weston holds a foreign commission, how can he command men of the U.S. Marines?* Weston doesn't care to explain. Though much about his mission is mysterious, he is rumored to have the backing of President Jefferson himself. Certainly he has the backing of someone: he has paid $19,000 in Venetian sequins, Spanish dollars, and British sterling to assemble and provision his army.

In his tent, Weston keeps a table and three chairs, a chest of clothing, and a trunk full of maps and official correspondence. Also a number of books—a collection the marines refer to as the Library of Alexandria. He has Emmerich de Vatel's *The Law of Nations,* in more or less pristine condition; Buffon's *Natural History*; Cochrane's *The Assassin Cults of Syria,* considerably thumbed; *A History of the Captivity and Suffering of Mrs. Josephine Froggatt, Who Was Six Years a Slave in Algiers*; and *A Collection of Songs, Selected from the Works of Mr. Dibdin, to Which are Added the Newest and Most Festive American Patriotic Airs.*

The general makes all of these tomes available to the men, on a limited basis. This works well. There is limited demand. Indeed, only Privates Sweet and Stennett have been spotted with books, and even they know better than to advertise their proclivities.

From the Diary of Lemuel Sweet, March 13, 1805

*We camp tonight at Borg al-Arab—literally, the "Arab's Tower."
This structure is an immense ruin of white stone, said to echo
in its lines the legendary lighthouse that stood in Alexandria's
harbor millennia ago. From this point on, everything in front
of us is waste—and a fearsome waste, at that. The Western
Desert is said to be haunted by the dead in life. Indeed, it is
difficult to contemplate the territory we are entering without
succumbing occasionally to flights of fancy.*

*By all outward appearances the land is empty, but lo, look
closer, and one sees, through the mists of history, the souls of
soldiers from a hundred nations, driven by steel and starvation
across the dunes, mingling with slave merchants in their camel
caravans, herding before them weeping companies of dust-
stained human chattel. Dealers in ivory and salt creep along
the trade routes, wary always of ambush. Muttering sorcerers
and sun-addled marabouts—Mahometan holy men—stagger
filthy and semi-naked through the wilderness like revenants
risen from an earth that welcomed them once but only to suck
all but bone and hair from their bodies before returning them
to the desperate carnival of the animate. Here the leprous,
shunned by family and faith, crawl out marred and obscene
from beneath rock ledges to show themselves to the morning sun,
as if in remonstration meek and unexpectant. Strange small
processions of nationless fire worshippers—Zoroastrians, driven
by the Turks from their ancestral homes in Persia—travel the
land in the darkest hours, disappearing at dawn, dreading
exposure of their secret creed.*

*The territory encourages abstraction. It holds no soft or
verdant corners, and thus perhaps no place for compromise or
comfort. Its history is a litany of bloody conflicts. Once in this
land the Hebrews spilled out of their mud cities instructed by
the words of their unnamable Deity to massacre the idolatrous.
Led by a man named Andreas, they killed Romans and*

Greeks alike. They cooked the flesh of their enemies, made belts of their entrails, fashioned their skins into clothing. Many of the foreigners they sawed in two, from the head downwards. Others they fed to wild beasts and still others were forced to fight each other in hastily constructed rings that mocked the might and pomp of northern empire. In all twenty thousand men, women, and children perished at the hands of the Jews. Whole cities were pulled down, stone by stone, and the inscriptions on their temples chiseled out as if to erase from mortal memory all traces of the gentile stain. Through these same parched lowlands many years later the messengers of Islam rode west, preaching obedience to the words of the Prophet. They brought all of North Africa under the flag of the crescent moon and indeed pushed deep into Europe before they were stopped by Charles the Hammer in steep valleys black with blood. This country remains theirs, at least in daylight hours. Mahometan pilgrims make their slow way east to the shrines of Mecca—the Masjid al-Haram, the Zamzam Well—on foot or by camel, and afterwards home.

Herodotus wrote that the Persian emperor Cambyses lost an entire army in this region, centuries before either Christ or Mohammed appeared on earth. Fifty thousand officers, infantrymen, and animals marched west from Egypt and were never heard from again. No man has ever been able to tell how they died or where their bodies lie. Perhaps the desert consumed them. The sand here moves like a sea, in massive eddies and currents. The earth itself shifts shape. The ancients believed the land to be home to gorgons and fallen forests of stone. This is where Hera cursed Lamia, and turned the beautiful girl into a fiend who devoured her children. It is said that the spiders of Cyrenaica grow as big as dogs, and can kill a man by spitting poison in his face.

Historians of old, convinced that monsters and giants roamed the many dark places of the world, nevertheless agreed that the Western Desert was the worst place on earth, and the things within it dangerous and unclean. Such phantasms no longer trouble our minds. But having banished superstition from the equation, it is nevertheless still necessary to acknowledge the very tangible perils posed by this barren expanse. Now, in the service of our new nation and our valiant General, eight Marines have come to test ourselves against it! I dare say we shall all be in somewise altered by the undertaking.

5.

Reinforcements

Three days later, aching and sunburnt, the expedition camps on a bluff overlooking the Mediterranean. Private Sweet descends a set of carved stone steps to wash his face in the ocean. He hears one of Prince Ahmad's men calling the Mahometans to prayer. In the distance a sea spout gyrates on the waves. Its dance is slow and silent, almost sensual. Or dangerous: like the swaying of the cobras Sweet saw in the markets of Alexandria.

The sky goes orange and pink. He will write about this in his diary. He will describe the shapes of the dunes. And the smell of the goats.

Sometime during the night a musket, ninety cartridges, and a cartouche box disappear from the magazine tent. Senor Rivera reports at first light that the sanctity of his tent has been violated as well. He seems agitated, though he declines to say what has been taken from him. A quick inventory reveals that eight of the general's cheeses are also missing. Doctor Rizzolo is unsurprised. The Arabs, he says, are natural thieves. They are as quiet as smoke.

Lieutenant Corrigan is furious. Henceforth the marines will sleep with their muskets beside them. Informed of the crimes, General Weston orders the army to segregate itself: Christians in one camp, Mahometans in the other. There is much discussion about the Egyptians. Most are Copts. *Christians*, Rizzolo explains, separated from communion with the West by metaphysical controversies rampant fourteen centuries earlier. The Council of Chalcedon. The Nestorian Heresy. The conflict centered on the Egyptian notion of Christ as one hypostasis in two natures. Largely incomprehensible to the layman—here the good doctor casts a dubious eye on the Americans—the dispute led to widespread violence and a permanent schism between Alexandria and Rome. Though the Alexandrian infantrymen are mercenaries, they hope to be the first Christians allowed to serve in Egypt's regular army under the liberal rule of the new *wali*, Muhammad Ali. They are looking for a battle to prove their worth. Unfortunately, Corrigan remains skeptical of both their competence and their commitment to the cause of liberty. The Egyptians are therefore ordered to camp with neither the Western Christians nor the followers of the Prophet, but somewhere in between.

"And none of your Nestorian hogwash," says the lieutenant. "There's only one true church, and it if it was good enough for Jesus, it's damn sure good enough for you."

✳ ✳ ✳

This evening the expedition is reinforced by Bedouin warriors led by the Sheikh Al Tahib, a tall tribesman with a broad forehead and a dark beard that extends halfway down his sternum. The sheikh arrives with a fanfare of ram's horns and a dozen black flags billowing above the heads of his cavalry. He brings ninety-seven men to fight for Prince Ahmad. These wild Arabs wrap themselves in long shirts and head cloths dyed russet-brown with the juice of a desert shrub. They are slightly built but trained to incredible endurance. Mounted on their swift, small-headed horses, they ride as if born in the saddle. Sweet senses they are tense with nervous energy, vigorously controlled.

"Bred from the purest race in the world," observes Colonel Ladendorf. Reflected sunlight flashes from his spectacles. The little Dutchman is much underfoot. He is curious about everything. The Bill of Rights. Von Steuben's Manual. The length of Long Island. He tells complicated stories with no apparent point or moral precept. He sings songs in languages none can decipher. Sweet is impressed by the size of his head. It is significantly larger than average—particularly the upper third of the skull. If one is to believe the writings of Franz Joseph Gall, the Dutchman's cranial chamber must house a particularly vigorous brain. "They live under conditions where only the hardiest and best survive."

Sweet studies the wild tribesmen: their dark eyes and flashing teeth and liquid, feral movements. "Are we sure they're on our side?" he asks.

But Ladendorf has already moved on. Sweet hears him chuckle. The sound is a hollow rasp, like reeds in a dried-up creek bed.

"Steadfast allies!" the colonel calls over his shoulder. "As long as your money holds out."

From the Diary of Lemuel Sweet,
March 19, 1805

It occurs to me that I have so far named but a few of the men with whom I march. I shall now rectify this oversight. First of course is my friend Donald Henry MacLeish, mentioned on several occasions in my shipboard journal and once already in these pages, a large man of impressive muscularity and strength, with the chest and shoulders of a Pennsylvania plow horse. Also in the company: Benjamin S. S. Stennett, a ginger-haired southerner from South Carolina, a prodigious wag-tongue who has at various times called himself journalist, farmer, and shopkeeper, tho by his own admission he was no great shakes at any of these professions; Moses Clay of Philadelphia, lean of form and feature, with bulging blue eyes and a jaw like a jackfish; Morris O'Dell, a banty rooster of a man from Chesapeake Bay, much given to balladry and the pursuit of what he calls dark-eyed women of the evening; Repentance Moore, the expedition's rifle man, tight-lipped and humorless, a westerner from Sorrowful Creek in Virginia; Stephen Prejean, a diminutive Mainer of French-Canadian lineage, possessed of a twisted right leg, & perhaps overly fond of cartooning; Hollis Miles Mason, oldest among us, a myopic drunkard who carries a Shawnee tomahawk and boasts of his prowess in close-quarters combat; and Lemuel Sweet—that is, I—youngest of the company, fair-haired & above the average in height, slightly stoop-shouldered I admit but blessed with sound teeth and good lungs. It is said that I am a star gazer, an impractical fellow. Perhaps it is so. I am nineteen years and almost four months old, and I confess that I have so far been unable to tie even so simple a knot as the clove hitch without close supervision. I suspect that I am not much trusted by my comrades, though I believe I am liked. I try at all times to listen more than I talk, as I was instructed by my mother, & to avoid hasty expressions of disapproval. In consequence of such, men tell me things.

I am pleased to report that we have made a friend at last among the foreigners. The man we call the Scarecrow, an Egyptian who acts as the general's interpreter, has deigned to visit with us as he practices his English. The position of interpreter is important to our endeavor, as the interpreter is the nexus, as it were, of all communications among the various contingents of the army. Our Scarecrow is a small-headed, spidery creature, & winced to much comical effect when he attempted to hoist one of our packs. But he is game enough, & won favorable notice from some of the Marines for his willingness to teach us rudiments of the Turkish lingo. Arkadas, he says, means friend. Help is yardim. The Egyptian soldiers we march with are not particularly friendly, tho they seem willing hands. The Greeks, on the other hand, are downright dismissive. They feign ignorance of our Revolution, and choose to call us English, tho corrected on this point multiple times. It seems indeed that the Greeks prefer to compare themselves with the Arabs, whom they strive to rival in feats of mischief and recklessness. For their part the Bedouin lancers who ride with the Sheikh al-Tahib look at us as upon the bearers of a loathsome disease, as perhaps they in their darkness believe the truths of Science and Philosophy to be.

Mostly we Americans keep to ourselves. It is our right & duty, says the Lieutenant, to lead these wild peoples by the example of our discipline & honor. In this regard I believe him to be exactly right. Such traits shall, more than any mere words, be the instruments of our instruction, and win us the affections of those with whom we come into contact. But even so the sentiment misses one of the most important boons attendant on our coming, for we bring in addition the blessings of Reason and the Rational Mind, which have done so much to accelerate the Progress of the Westerner in his home and abroad.

Much commotion among the dogs last night. I suspect a battle of some sort took place, as two of their number are no longer to be seen, while the others bear livid scars. I would try to treat them, but they are too scared to let me approach.

6.

The Rightful Ruler

Ahmad Vartoonian says he is the true king of Tripoli by all the laws of God and man. He just needs a little help in convincing his subjects. Ahmad is a pear-shaped individual with oiled hair, large lips, and brown eyes tending to black. A mole grows in the center of his forehead, just above his nose.

Prince Ahmad

His chin is delicately formed but marred by a long scar where he was branded as a child to cure some infirmity or illness, and he has small white teeth that rarely show, for he seldom smiles. His gloom is understandable. His younger brother, Yusuf, wants him dead. Yusuf lured their father to a secret meeting, where he shot him in the throat, then chopped the old man into a dozen pieces. He tried to poison Ahmad a month later, but killed Ahmad's wife instead. (*A pity*, the usurper later admitted. *She had always been kind.*) Ahmad fled—first to Malta, and then to Egypt. He wears silks and an ornate Yemeni dagger. An emerald flashes from his turban. He is a sleepy-eyed man, ruled by rumors and much given to suspicion. Outside his tent stands a wooden pole with the horse-hair streamer that marks him as a man of distinction among the Turks. This is to confuse potential assassins; most nights Ahmad sleeps elsewhere. Of the Americans he will speak only to Weston. Weston has made him sign a contract that the general, typically grandiose, calls a "convention." In return for U.S. financial and military assistance in reclaiming the throne of Tripoli from his younger brother, Prince Ahmad will release the crew of the *Charleston* from their captivity in the Red Fortress. In addition, there will be no more tributes exacted from American shipping. Piracy will cease, except insofar as it involves vessels of the Asiatic nations and possibly France. And Yusuf Vartoonian's son-in-law, the red-bearded Scottish corsair who converted to Mahometanism and now calls himself Murad Reis, will be turned over to the U.S. Navy for disciplinary proceedings befitting a common criminal. In short, the insolent bastard will be hanged from the nearest yardarm.

"Furtherwise," muses Private Stennett to his comrades, wiping his wooden spoon in the sand, "all deserving marines will receive, upon demand, smartly delivered, one or more willing and suitably formed native females. For immediate usage."

"With such females to be practiced in the Parisian arts," says Private O'Dell. Sewing a button to the sleeve of his jacket.

"And free of the pox."

"And able to drive tent pegs," adds Hollis Mason. "Remember the important things."

"Truly the General is an able negotiator."

"But not such a smart one. Who'd negotiate with that rheumy ol' bastard?"

"Who?" says O'Dell.

"Ahmad, that's who. Prince Ahmad the Plump."

"Ahmad the Plump just happens to be the true king of Tripoli. That's who we're fighting for, simpleton."

O'Dell snorts. "And him as soft as suet. No wonder they kicked him out. *Wiped him off,* is more like it."

"All the same," says MacLeish. "It's him you'll be spilling your guts for, if the general has his way."

The big man has a talent for ending argument. It's not just his words. It's also their delivery, which comes with just enough force that his listeners can detect the reservoir of resentment beneath it. Still, it's a point worth remembering. The marines have come to this country to fight. And some, no doubt, to die.

7.

The Temple of Ammon

The expedition is a long, slow, many-legged creature that drags a plume of dust behind it like a tail. Today the marines march west eighteen miles into a low sand valley and then up across the desert plains to encounter their first set of ruins: a collection of columns and walls, and what might have been a modest amphitheater, all gutted by time, like a set of Greek skeletons adrift on an ocean of sand.

"Two thousand years old, boys," says Benjamin Stennett. The former schoolteacher enjoys displaying his superior fund of knowledge. He has some Latin. He has traveled widely in New Hampshire.

Sweet attempts to put the number in perspective. He thinks of the date of his birth. The Magna Carta. The Fall of Rome. According to Bishop Ussher's scientific calculations, two thousand years is fully one third the length of the world's existence.

"Alexander the Great came this way to visit the oracle of Jupiter Ammon," Stennett notes.

Private Clay adjusts his trousers. The column has halted for the day, and the marines sit in the shade of a wall of rock.

"Ammon?"

Stennett takes a long drink from his canteen. "The supreme deity in these parts. At least back in those days. Body of a man. Head of a ram."

"Why?"

"Why what?"

"Why'd this codger care to talk to a sheep man?"

"A ram," Stennett explains, running a hand through his red hair. The Southerner is fair-skinned, and has been badly burned by the sun. "Not a sheep. And not even to the ram. To the ram god's priests. Alexander had conquered the world. He wondered if—"

"He never conquered Philadelphia," says Clay. His eyes are so prominent that every glance seems like an accusation.

"There wasn't no Philadelphia, addlepate."

"What's that supposed to mean?"

"He means it was ages ago," says Stennett. "Philadelphia's a whelping brat by comparison."

"So why are we talking about it?"

"Because Alexander took this here road we're traveling now."

"That just means," MacLeish mutters, "he was as stupid as we are."

"Alexander," says Colonel Ladendorf, "thought he was a god." *Gott*, it sounds like. "Never defeated in battle. Conqueror, as you have said, of the known world."

The marines exchange glances. The Dutchman has not been asked to join the parley. Even shipboard, enlisted men have no obligation to include a gentleman in their conversation. And yet Ladendorf is an officer, and some measure of respect is certainly due.

"And was he?" asks Prejean, to break the silence. "A *god*, I mean?"

Ladendorf shrugs. "So the oracle said. Alas, the great king died not long afterward. His claim to divinity suffered from this development. His body was anointed in honey and laid in a sarcophagus shaped to his form, which was in turn placed in a golden casket and draped in purple robes. King Ptolemy stole the body and brought it to Alexandria, where it lay on display for many decades. Ptolemy IX, an unlucky king, and very foolish, replaced Alexander's sarcophagus with a glass one, and melted the golden casket in order to strike an issue of coins in his own image. The citizens of Alexandria took offense. Soon afterward a group of them, many hundreds strong, seized Ptolemy as he walked in the street. They tore him limb from limb, stuck his head on a pole, and planted it in the center of the city for the birds to feed upon. The metropolis was gripped by a sort of madness in those days. There were riots and murders. Livestock delivered dead offspring, and the moon refused to rise. Alexander's whereabouts have remained unknown from that time to this. So perhaps he was a god after all. Yes? Do we not *kill* for our gods? And do they not hide from us when we call?"

Ladendorf concludes this address with open arms, grinning as if to invite an affirmative response. When none is offered, the colonel moves on. Even the air feels old. There is something odd about the Dutchman. The tawny, lion-skinned color of his eyes, for example. Is this even possible? Sweet is reluctant to judge. Before enlisting in the marines, seven months earlier, he had never left Massachusetts. In the time since, he's seen a few things: Men with no legs. A two-headed calf. A woman in Malta who wheeled her own abdominal tumor in front of her in a hand cart. But he has never known a person to have eyes of this hue. And the man's movements. *Jerky*, as if recently learned. The colonel is like an instrument gone out of tune, slightly off, lending whatever conversation he joins a faint but unmistakable dissonance.

"Queer sort," says Clay.

"Only the best," says MacLeish, "for General Weston's army."

"He's got a lot of stories," Repentance Moore observes.

"Every lunatic has stories. Visit the cranky hutch and you'll have a dozen for dinner."

"The Arabs don't like him. Say he smells funny."

"They should talk. Funny how?"

"Like knives. Or knife *blades*. They say he smells like metal."

"Aye? And how would you happen to know that?"

"Scarecrow told me. He don't like him neither."

O'Dell is the first to mention it. "He's took a fancy to you, Sweet."

Sweet is bent over his journal, sketching a distant cloud. He glances up, perplexed. "Who?"

"The Dutchman."

"What's that supposed to mean?"

No one answers. But he knows. All his life, men have favored Sweet with their presence. He is a handsome youth, refreshingly frank, uncommonly well spoken. Colonel Ladendorf has several times chosen to walk with Sweet and MacLeish at the rear of the column. It is an act of remarkable condescension. Highly unorthodox. The colonel speaks with both of the marines, but he is clearly more interested in the younger man. The birdlike Dutchman never ceases to ask questions. Sweet welcomes his company at first. He mentions his upbringing in New England and his desire to study natural history at the conclusion of his enlistment. He speaks of his mother and of his unfortunate little sister, Clara, a beautiful child who was born simple and who will never be able to live by herself. Sweet tells Ladendorf also of the American experiment—of a new kind of government, created by and for the governed themselves. President Washington put it best. The United States is a nation that wants no foreign dominions, only to be left alone to cultivate the fruits of liberty.

The colonel listens intently. Something about the young man's enthusiasm excites him. As he listens, a half-smile flickers across his narrow face. Almost as if he is agreeing, the colonel suggests that others have come to this region with prescriptions for enlightenment: wandering Greeks hauling behind them their marble pantheon of quarrelsome deities; Crusaders with the Holy Cross, that avenue through tears to perfect love and mercy; *jihadis* screaming the words of the Prophet. And before them all the feverish incantations of pre-literate wanderers, terrified by any unlikely circumstance but like their descendants anxious always to be right and willing to bathe in the blood of others as testament to and validation of their certainties. It is this combination of viciousness and ignorance, the Colonel suggests, that made them human in the first place. Yes? Don't men distinguish themselves from the rest of creation primarily by their talent for destroying each other in the name of invisible deities? The little Dutchman gestures. The efficacy of the preachments of all these peoples, he says, can be seen in every direction: sand, and sun, and walls of crumbling stone.

Sweet is not the sort to argue. Nor does his rank give him leave to do so. He bites off the urge to contradict the colonel's cynicism. MacLeish, meanwhile, seems to find the conversation tedious. He does not care to curry favor with officers. He keeps his mouth shut and his eyes fixed forward. He has no interest in history. The big man has learned all he needs to know. By all appearances, he is more concerned with avoiding the leavings of the camels that walk in front of them. It is no easy job.

* * *

In the afternoon a courier arrives from the east. A dispatch from the U.S. Navy reached Alexandria shortly after Weston's departure, and Sir John Cholmondely has sent it on. Unfortunately the communique is made an addendum to Sir John's own musings, delivered in his usual rambling fashion. The Plague has been reported in Cairo again, he writes, and cholera is taking a terrible toll in the Levant. On the other hand, all signs point to a favorable cotton crop this year. And a rash of grisly killings in the Christian quarter of Alexandria—five girls murdered, and their bodies quite horribly disfigured—seems to have ceased around the time the expedition set out, leaving the residents greatly relieved. Finally the dispatch. An American frigate, *Endurance*, captured a Tripolitan merchant ship leaving Derna on March 6th. After questioning the vessel's officers and crew, *Endurance* reports that the citizens of Derna, having heard rumors of Prince Ahmad's return to Tripoli, have risen to support his claim to the throne. Musket fire can be heard in the streets. Governor Ali Rasmin, a favorite of King Yusuf, has barricaded himself in his palace.

Weston is delighted. Derna is ripe for the taking. He shares the news at once with Ahmad. In consequence of these great good tidings, the prince's supporters sound their horns and engage in feats of horsemanship and *feu de joie*. Unfortunately, the camel drivers hear the firing and fear the worst: an attack by the wild tribes of the desert, who materialize from the hills like ill will when and where they choose. As if by pre-designated signal, or perhaps by racial or religious reflex, the drivers draw their curved daggers. They vow to slit the throats of the Christian dogs who have led them to ambush. If they are to die, they say, at least they will die in *jihad*. They are restrained only by the entreaties of an Arab of some importance among them, who insists that prudence dictates they should suspend their bloody work till the cause of the firing is discovered, and all freighting fees paid.

The crisis is thus averted. All sheathe their weapons.

* * *

That night the army camps again near the sea. MacLeish finds two copper coins, their inscriptions so worn as to be unintelligible. Puzzlement and speculation follow the discovery. The Greeks are summoned. They recognize characters of their language, but cannot translate the message. Colonel Ladendorf intervenes. He says the image on the coin is that of King Ptolemy Apion, who died without an heir many centuries earlier and bequeathed this land to Rome. The letters read, *His Glory Shall Not Diminish.* MacLeish trades the coins to General Weston's translator, the tall Egyptian the marines call Scarecrow, in return for Turkish tobacco. Weston reckons they are five hundred miles from Derna. Word spreads through camp.

"Hear that?" says O'Dell. "Five hundred miles. We'll be there day after tomorrow."

"Hold your goddamned tongue," says MacLeish. "Or you ain't gonna get there at all."

Some men hate to walk.

* * *

Selim Comb, commander of the Egyptians, kills a leopard near her lair. He brings back the carcass, plus three sightless cubs. The mother is skinned and eaten. All judge the flesh to be adequate fare, though gristly. As the offspring are too young for either use or amusement, they are tossed into the fire. The marines agree not to tell Private Sweet about the dead cubs. The boy is impressionable. He takes things hard.

8.

Lost City of the Crusaders

By mid-morning Sweet and MacLeish have been up and moving for six hours. They are two weeks into the march and thinner already. Their hands and forearms are burnt red and peeling, and the skin of their lips is flaking off. They try not to look at the sky as the heat rolls murderous and huge in waves out of the yellow land.

Sweet's blisters bleed. His boots are Newcastle-made, sturdy but stiff. The marines wear blue woolen jackets with scarlet facings and high leather collars, and by noon the jackets are dark with sweat. Lieutenant Corrigan ignores the complaints of his men. He prohibits them from spitting. He says this is to allow them to conserve their internal moisture, but everyone knows he hates the habit. The lieutenant also insists that the marines' jackets remain on. Essential for order, he says. Impresses the natives. His only concession in this matter regards the men's hats. High-crowned and almost brimless, the hats are decorated with a plume of red plush on the front, a brass eagle and plate, and a band of blue and yellow silk. The lieutenant concedes their uselessness on the march. The marines are allowed to wear forage caps of blue wool instead.

The men's mood is somber. As long as their route runs in sight of the sea, all is well; the Mediterranean's breakers give the scene freshness and life. But the coast is irregular, and following the contours of its many capes and inlets would cost valuable time. Weston therefore veers inland. When the track bends southward and stretches away across the Sahara, the immense indifference of Africa descends upon the marines with a crushing weight. It feels wrong to point oneself into the heart of this bleak and unwelcoming mass.

The wind off the desert spits sand in their eyes. Dense flocks of songbirds are returning north. It is a normal event, but it seems to Sweet as if they flee some formless and unknowable thing that has awakened in the dark strange depths of the continent and now chases them to the sea. The men take shots at the heavens, then race to retrieve the few birds that fall to earth. It is a joyless hunt. The birds are bitter to the taste.

One marksman crosses a ridge in search of his kill and finds instead a fortress of crumbling stone. The walls of the deserted structure are sixteen feet high and five thick, with battlements on the curtain constructed for archers. The marines join the reconnaissance. *What was here to defend?* Sweet thinks. *And from whom?* No clue remains. Generally an optimist, Sweet nevertheless wonders if the first reflexive effort of those who settle in this land must always be to construct a means to hold what they own from the avarice and cunning of others.

Theft after theft.
World without end.

In the center of the ruined citadel is an immense cistern cut from the rock. It must have been supplied at one time by rain water conveyed to it from the terraces of buildings, as its depth is but thirty feet, and the only well of water in the vicinity is considerably deeper. But both the cistern and the well are dry. A bad omen. The heat has left the Christians parched and quarrelsome. The Spaniard is in especially bad shape. Sr. Rivera is an opium eater. His supply of laudanum has vanished, and Dr. Rizzolo has proven unwilling to part with even a portion of the meager of morphine in his pharmacopeia, in the belief that it may be needed by the ill and injured in the near future. A reasonable caution, no doubt—but Rivera is beyond reason. He threatens the doctor in Spanish and Latin with prolonged and hideous punishments. Sweet has heard Rivera's cries in the night. The man's dreams torment him. He has scratched great welts in his thighs and stomach, and his appearance in the daylight hours is horrific indeed. Pale and red-eyed, he shrinks from the sun. His dry tongue constantly crawls over his lips, searching for moisture, and he will not look at a mirror. He sweats profusely and has fallen twice from his horse.

Colonel Ladendorf in particular considers him an object of scorn. Sweet is unsure what to think. He avoids the man when possible. There is an air of ruin about Rivera, a promise of unwholesome secrets and unfortunate endings. He looks half dead already.

Around the fortress are ruins of ancient buildings of apparently excellent masonry, the cement of which greatly resembles that of the ruins of Carthage. Time in many places has consumed the freestone of the walls, leaving the cement intact but honey-combed, as if occupied by a race of giant insects. Scattered among these ruins are numerous graves of pilgrims. Rough-hewn headstones bear Turkish and Arabic inscriptions, some smeared almost to nothing by the elements, others expressive of little other than a name or place of origin. Barren desert stretches as far as the eye can see, seemingly never cultivated, yet here and there dotted with ruins standing like silent testaments to decline and defeat. *Hajis* passing in this vast expanse, desperate for any rudiment of communication, have built cairns beside the road. Sometimes they are individual piles of stones. Sometimes they are common heaps, to which any disposed passer-by might add his rock—not reasonably or with known motive, but because others did, and perhaps they knew.

✿ ✿ ✿

This evening the marines build a fire out of camel dung to boil their coffee. MacLeish and Stennett pack pipes and smoke their precious tobacco. Two fires over, the Greeks are singing. Private O'Dell will not be bettered. He starts with a favorite:

> *Come all you warriors and renowned nobles,*
> *Who once commanded brave warlike bands.*
> *Throw down your plumes and your golden trophies.*
> *Take up your arms with a trembling hand.*
> *For Father Murphy of the County Wexford,*
> *Lately roused from his sleepy dream,*
> *Has vowed to cut down cruel Saxon oppressors*
> *And wash them away in a crimson stream...*

"Goddamned Irish," mutters MacLeish. "If only they'd fight as fierce as they sing."

The melody fades. Stars drift overhead. Sirius, already close to setting. Orion. The Bear.

"Don't waste your time looking out yonder," says Moses Clay. He snaps his fingers in front of Sweet's face.

"Why not?"

"On account of there's nothin' out there, that's why not."

"There has to be something," says Sweet.

"Says who?"

"These people." Sweet gestures toward the Arab camp a hundred yards distant. A dozen small fires wink back at him. "They come from *somewhere.*"

"Sand and bones," says O'Dell. "Thousands of miles of it."

Repentance Moore is polishing his bayonet. The Virginian speaks so rarely that his words have added weight. Even MacLeish looks up. "And all without a map to guide a man. Can you credit that? Who lives in a country without a map?"

"There's Zerzura," offers Prejean. The cartoonist. Looking up from a drawing.

"Ze-who?"

"The lost oasis. Silver and gold. Legend has it, it's out there somewhere."

"Legend ain't payin' your wages," says O'Dell.

Prejean shrugs. "I ain't sure anyone's paying my wages."

"Tell it," says MacLeish. The big man places another lump of camel dung on the fire.

"They say it's down south," says Prejean. The curly-haired cartoonist cocks his head, as if trying to recall the details of a complicated set of instructions. "A white city. The main gate surmounted by the figure of a giant bird…"

"A turkey, most like," says Clay. But mildly. MacLeish laughs. "A turkey. I could find use for a turkey right about now."

"Stop your gob and eat your goat."

"…and cool water bubblin' out of the ground."

MacLeish: "Wild notions bubblin' out a' yer ass, more like. This whole country's cursed. Dry as your grannie's nethermouth. And you'd best keep a weather eye out for them camel humpers over yonder, lest they take a notion to stick a knife in your throat some starry night."

"We're already sleepin' on our muskets. What else is we supposed to do? Hide the bayonets up our asses?"

"The Corps expects every man to do his duty, Mr. O'Dell."

"*Tell*," MacLeish repeats, his voice grown thicker.

"Ask the sawbones," says Prejean. "Which told me."

"Sawbones ain't here. Looks like you're elected."

"All right. Fine. Doctor Rizzolo—which ain't here, and which is probably cupshot by now, playing at whist with the gentlemen—says once there was a salt caravan traveling west of here which was hit by a sandstorm. Storm lasted two days and a night. By the time it settled, the caravan, humans and camels alike, had died of suffocation. Only one man, a camel driver called Hamid, crawled out from underneath the dead animals and looked out across the sand. Hamid climbed a hill to get a view of the desert, but the storm had changed the landscape so as he couldn't recognize nothing. He struggled along the scarp hoping he could get his bearings, but it was no use. He started walking north, into the face of the wind, thinking he could make it to the coast. He was parched just about dead when he was found by a crowd of blokes the likes of which he'd never clapped eyes on before. Fair-haired they were, and blue-eyed. What's more, they carried straight swords, not these bent-up back-scratchers the Bedoos fancy. When he later found his way to a city—Benghazi, I think the doctor said—the camel driver related his story to whoever would listen. But he always seemed shifty in the telling."

"Shifty? Like Stennett?"

Prejean grins. "A little. Aye. But without the Grecian tendencies."

Stennett looks up. "Jackanapes. See if you get any more baccy from me. What was the camel driver's story, then?"

"Hamid said the strange men lived in a city in the desert called Zerzura. There they took him after the sand storm, half-dead as he was, and cared for him till he recovered. The little village was beautifully tended. Vines and palms sprouted in every corner. Access was by a wadi that ran between two mountains, and from it a road proceeded to the gates of the city, which was walled to the height of three men. Or two MacLeishes. Above the gate was the bird I mentioned, and the houses inside the walls were white in the sun. Water was plentiful, and pools and springs were used by slender light-skinned women and their children for washing and bathing. The men were tall and warlike, with freckled skin and tawny beards. The dwellings were richly furnished. The people of Zerzura spoke a passable Arabic, but with many peculiar words the camel driver couldn't understand until they was carefully explained to him. The strange people were evidently not Mahometans, because the women went unveiled, and Mr. Hamid saw no mosque, and heard no muezzin."

"What's a *muezzin*?"

"He's the quid what goes up in the tower and starts screeching about Allah."

"He tells the people to say their prayers," says Sweet.

"Five times a day, Lord love 'em."

"That's when they stick their noses in the dirt and talk to the devil?" asks Clay. A Methodist, he is not shy about advertising his convictions in religious matters.

"They're not talking to the devil," says Sweet. "The Scarecrow says they're demonstrating submission to the will of God. Their god, anyway."

"There ain't but one God, Sweetie. If they want to talk to Him, they need to look up, not down. Everyone knows that."

MacLeish interjects: "Let him finish the yarn, boys."

"The local prince—what they call a *emir* in these parts—heard tell of Hamid's story. He had the camel driver brought before him, and he asked the poor sod how he come to be in Benghazi. Hamid didn't much like the question. Did some squirming, like as not, but he was compelled to answer nevertheless. He said he escaped from Zerzura one night when he'd recovered his humors, and after a difficult journey north made his way to the city. The emir was puzzled, and wondered why it was necessary to escape this wonderful place unless he was being held a prisoner. The camel driver started sweating, and couldn't explain why his story was inconsistent, him having swore up and down that his rescuers were kind. The emir thereupon ordered his guards to search the unlucky bastard. They discovered in his robes a huge, flawless ruby set in a gold ring. Asked how he come by such a stone, the camel driver was unable to give a straight answer.

The emir reckoned Hamid had pinched it from people who had shown him great kindness, which is a sin among the Arabs."

"It ain't exactly high praise among the rest of us, you know."

"Then and there the emir had the poor beggar's hands lopped off, which is what you might call the standard issue punishment for thieves in these parts."

"I seen 'em done like that in Alexandria," says O'Dell. "Their clampers cut off and hung round their necks on a string. Seen 'em beggin' out in—"

"We all seen it. And some with their tongues yanked out, for speaking ill of their prophet. Let him finish the goddamned story."

"And so poor Hamid profited little from his deeds. Rizzolo says the ruby ring was owned for many years by the emir. It was examined by the Jews of Benghazi, who said it was of immense value. More important, they declared it to be of a workmanship unknown to them, and many centuries old. Judging from the markings on the inside of the band, some said it was a ring that belonged to Solomon, the greatest of the Hebrew kings, and that it was an object of terrible power and magic. A *talisman*, they called it. Enchanted—and very dangerous in evil hands. When the ring went missing, stolen from inside the palace, the emir was so chapped, he killed a Jew every day for thirty-four days until he learned his prize might be somewhere else."

Sweet speaks up. "A Jew every day? Why the Jews?"

"On account of it was the Jews who knew what the ring might be. And what made it so valuable. He figured they was the ones who'd want to pinch it."

"Makes sense. And did they?"

"No one knows. Some say it couldn't have been stole by a mortal man, on account of it was under guard, like. And no one in the palace had disappeared—just the ring. It was rumored to be here and there over the years. Some said it was returned to Zerzura for a time, and then stole again, and all the inhabitants of the place left for dead. But to get back to the story: Rizzolo says these Zerzura characters was the descendants of Crusaders who pilfered holy items from the catacombs beneath the great temple of Jerusalem. As a consequence of their theft, and many great blasphemies besides, God caused them to become lost in the Western desert as they made their way home. So these knights and their consorts, their children and their children's children, have lived ever since in this tiny oasis, smack dab in the arse end of nowhere. Some Crusaders did get lost on the way out to the Holy Land, or back from it. It's wrote up in the books, says the doctor, and it don't seem like a hard thing to do, once you've seen the Sahara. So that's who these coves is. Or *was*. Lost knights, in a city called Zerzura, hid from the world and condemned, like, to guard the treasures they stole. No one gets in. But if they ever did get in, and then back out, they'd be rich. Rich as bloody Croesus."

"And if they *didn't* get out?" says Stennett. "They'd be dead. Dead as old Louie Capet."

"Dead as Alexander Hamilton," says Mason. The oldest of the marines is a known Republican, and set in his ways. His jibe goes unanswered. The temperature drops quickly in the desert. The men wrap their jackets around themselves and roll out their blankets. The fires die as the hours pass. Private Sweet stands the middle watch. Nothing stirring this night. Straight through till dawn. And then a reluctant sun, as if gathering its strength. But more to come, it promises. And soon.

"This is no place for a white man," says Clay, rubbing sleep from his eyes.

"This is no place for *any* man," says Stennett.

And no one contradicts him.

9.

A Disturbing Discovery

The column is half a mile long, and a dozen of Sheikh al-Tahib's young warriors have claimed the lead. They gallop their horses ahead and then come pounding back, enthused by their own vitality, aflame with the prospect of battle. They claim to see a body of cavalry on the horizon to the southwest, and several times attempt to make contact with it. But these phantom horsemen are elusive. They seem to melt into the desert each time the sheikh's riders approach. After three mornings in a row of these sightings, the excitement in the column subsides. An illusion, Dr. Rizzolo opines. A figment of the imagination attributable to over-excitement and the relentless heat.

Weston and Prince Ahmad ride together most days, accompanied by their aides and the gentlemen. Six of the marines follow immediately behind them on foot. Corrigan's orders are to keep the general always in sight. Yusuf Karamanli is known to employ skillful assassins, and the murder of General Weston would do almost as much as the death of Ahmad himself to end the dangers posed to King Yusuf by the expedition.

Immediately behind the marines comes the prince's household, an oily collection of panderers and honeyfugglers in brightly colored tunics and turbans, all eager to demonstrate the closeness of their relationship with the future king. Then come the riotous Greeks, squat, muscular men in scarlet *kepis*, fustanella kilts, and long socks and sandals; next, the murmuring Egyptians, clad in white linen save for their black ammunition belts and khaki field caps; and after this the baggage train, the mobile kitchen, cooks and stewards, the camels and goats, the drivers and the drivers' families—women and children, the elderly and infirm. Random dogs pad along in pursuit, looking deflated and ashamed. Dogs have no honor in this land. Most go unnamed, save for the rough epithets—Ripper; Worm Bait; The Wriggler—applied to them by the marines. Sweet and Prejean leave out food for the animals, a habit that elicits scorn from the Arabs and rebukes from Lieutenant Corrigan.

Sheikh al-Tahib travels at a distance from Weston's column, sometimes ahead, at others behind. The sheikh is said to be mercurial and violent. He fancies himself cousin to the desert's birds of prey. An avid falconer, he occasionally reminds his followers that he is to be known as the Hawk. He rides a jet black stallion, seated in a Spanish saddle adorned with blue velvet and strings of turquoise beads. He has a flag of his own, white Arabic script on a background of black, and it pleases him to make no show of obedience to the Christians. He is of a southern tribe noted for its piety. Colonel Ladendorf reports that the sheikh brought his men to the expedition partly to avenge a kinsman who acted as imam to a group of Salafists in Derna. The governor of the province, Ali Rasmin, had the imam thrown in prison, where he died under suspicious circumstances. Ali Rasmin is profane and superstitious, disdainful of sharia law. He consorts with Shiites and Jews. The sheikh intends to teach him a lesson. Still, the atmosphere in the American camp grows tense whenever the Hawk appears. Though he is nominally an ally of General Weston, and has been paid handsomely for his services, the sheikh behaves as if he has happened upon the Christians in this vast desert wholly by chance, and is not entirely pleased by the meeting.

* * *

This morning Sweet and MacLeish march again in the rear, with the livestock. The sounds are the soft thuds of the camels' feet, the curses of the drivers, the crack of a whip. Occasionally a group of the sheikh's men will drop back to survey the tail end of the column. It is dusty here, so they don't stay long. They ride by the two marines and gaze appraisingly at their uniforms, their weapons. They speak to each other as if the Americans are not men at all, but rather beasts devoid of sense and thus incapable of taking offense or even notice.

"Sizing us up," says MacLeish. They are far enough away from Lieutenant Corrigan that the big man marches with his jacket unbuttoned. "I think that one-eyed quid wants your Springfield."

"Where?"

"There to larboard. The Cyclops."

Sweet shrugs his shoulder to adjust the weight of his musket. The Springfield Model 1795 is a .69 caliber flintlock, fully five feet in length. It weighs ten pounds if it weighs an ounce, and is accurate to seventy-five yards, but only with a steady hand and little wind. "He'll have to take that up with the lieutenant. Captain Watson made him swear his life out as guaranty for return of the muskets before we left the ship."

"He's a bold one. I'll grant him that."

"Watson?"

"The Arab. *Cyclops.* Hard to tell, with them robes and all, but he looks fair built."

"Can he not put a patch on that empty socket?" Sweet asks. "Seems like sand would get in it."

"Musket ball, more like. I'll put one right between his wattles if he keeps staring."

"Maybe he thinks you're staring at him."

"Oh, aye. On account of I am. And I'm wondering what he's man enough to do about it. Remember that Limey tar back in Portsmouth?"

"He was just about the same size," says Sweet.

"And him with both his peepers. Said you was too pretty to be a soldier, didn't he? But he went down easy enough."

"He was stumbling drunk. And he did manage to take something of yours."

MacLeish chuckles. He is the kind of man who finds his own misbehavior amusing. "Took it straight to hell, I reckon.

I wasn't using that ear anyhow. And I didn't pour the grog down his throat."

"That you did not. But the Arabs don't drink."

"One of their many vices, Sweetie." MacLeish leans over as if to spit, but thinks better of it. "They sleep, don't they?"

"What's that supposed to mean?"

The big man wraps one arm around Sweet and pulls him close. "It means you need to stick with me, son, if you know what's good for you. The honest are always abused by the wicked."

Sweet can't help but grin. In this vast wasteland it is reassuring to know he can count on at least one of the men around him.

* * *

In the afternoon the column climbs up onto a featureless gravel plain that drains to the sea. Here on a scorched brown bluff the sheikh's scouts find crude shelters with roofs of driftwood and tamarind branches, supported by pillars of piled stones. All are empty. In the center of this rough circle of structures sit two lines of brass helmets, very old, configured as if for advance. Another mystery. None can say who built these habitations, or where the residents have gone. A spring trickles out from the limestone. Women from the column water the camels and fill goatskins from the spring. One of the women—a girl, really—has stained her face green. Another has daubed blue and yellow stripes on her cheeks, and wears a hoop of gold through her right nostril. She reaches up to touch Sweet's blonde hair. She looks into his eyes as she loops a finger through one of his curls. When the private blushes, the girl laughs, leans into her friend, and starts back toward the herdsmen's camp.

"Another one that fancies you," says Private O'Dell. It is a recognized phenomenon. Women find Sweet an object of humor and delight. O'Dell surveys his companion from toe to crown. His brown eyes show confusion, envy, and a certain pride of affiliation. "I reckon it's the hair. 'Cause it ain't like you'd know what to do with one of them tarts."

Sweet ignores the remark, which contains just enough truth to sting. He reminds himself there will be plenty of time to learn such secrets. He also believes there is a right way and a wrong way to handle this matter, and that losing his innocence to a dockside whore, as he has been advised to do on more than one occasion, is probably not the best method. What's more, the prospect scares him. He suspects he will measure up, but how can a man be sure?

* * *

Next day the marines circulate Stephen Prejean's latest cartoon. The little Mainer is an avid artist. He stands just over five feet, and his lopsided gait has made the journey difficult, but he is often seen smiling. He lost one of his pencils only a day out of Alexandria. The other has worn down almost to nothing. Prejean uses charcoal instead. He tears pages from the general's encyclopedia or, if nothing else is available, sketches on the canvas of the tents. He could charge for his caricatures, if his companions had any money. In his idle moments he depicts THE DEATH OF COLUMBIA AT THE HANDS OF JEFFERSON AND THE REPUBLICANS, and THE DEPREDATIONS OF JEAN CRAPEAU ON THE HIGH SEAS, CHALLENGED ONLY BY THE VALIANT U.S. MARINES.

Today he has drawn the fabled city of Zerzura as a domed metropolis with a giant bird perched on its central gate. At the terminus of its featherless neck, the bird has the face of the expedition's purported leader, Prince Ahmad. Its croak is transcribed in a sound balloon that stands nearly vertical above the bird's head: *Welcome, U.S. Marines. Your Muskets are welcome but your Money is not. Please visit our Undergd. Rivers of Beer and similar nourishing Refreshmts. All gratis!* An officer that looks like Lieutenant Corrigan observes from one corner of the drawing. His jacket is buttoned and his boots are neatly polished. He clearly disapproves of the proceedings. General Weston is visible in the opposite corner, chasing butterflies with an oversized net. Sweet is mildly scandalized to learn that his fellow marines have come to suspect Weston is an impractical fellow, a high-minded ponce who pursues abstractions through the heat. Sweet is offended by such talk—mostly because he is fond of the same abstractions. When the general speaks of liberty, Sweet can almost see it floating on the horizon. He believes in the blessings of democracy and representative government. In fact he holds out hope that no fighting will be necessary in Cyrenaica. So many natives will rally to the banners of America and her political favorite, Prince Ahmad, that King Yusuf will be forced from his throne without a shot being fired. If this is to be a war of ideas, Sweet thinks, surely the marines are better armed.

* * *

The Scarecrow is dead.

Two of the Greeks find the body near a shallow privy just after sunrise. The news spreads quickly through camp. Sweet follows the crowd. He sees that the back of the Egyptian's skull is smashed and sticky, clotted with sand. His eyes are missing, having been removed from his head with no apparent precision. His partially eaten liver, kidneys, and heart are found nearby, evidently scooped out of the torso through a gaping hole just below the left side of the rib cage. His knife and sandals have also been taken. Private Moore finds these items a few hundred yards to the east. The eyes as well. They have been set down beside each other as if still functional, and arranged to suggest that they are staring back along the route the army has traveled thus far.

The gangling Egyptian stood almost six feet tall but weighed no more than seven stone. Formerly a porter in the Mameluke army of Murad Bey, the Scarecrow was a man of exemplary habits. All agree that he showed considerable aptitude for the languages of the West, English in particular. Indeed, after some tutoring from Private O'Dell, even his profanities were apt. Speculation runs to animal predation. Dr. Rizzolo opines that the wound was not made by a blade. It is too ragged and imprecise. Rather, the aperture looks like the work of claws or teeth. There are spotted cats in the desert, and jackals have been known to range this far north in the winter months. On the other hand, why would jackals make off with a man's knife and sandals? Others argue that bandits have struck. The desert harbors desperate men. Yet here the fact that the knife and sandals were left *behind*, not far from the body, plays a part. Why kill except for profit? And what enemy could the Scarecrow have had in this lonely place? While there are no tracks nearby, the terrain is mostly rock, and the wind has been at work, erasing all traces of human and animal transit.

It is a crisis. The murder is troubling, of course, but General Weston has bigger concerns on his mind. He suddenly finds himself without a translator. Other members of the expedition can speak both Arabic and English, but only one among them also knows Berber.

Fortunately, Colonel Ladendorf is pleased to be of service.

From the Diary of Lemuel Sweet, March 25, 1805

Before I saw it for myself, I could scarcely have formed a conception of the vastness of this place, & its harshness to all forms of Life. In portions of the desert great systems of Dunes have developed. They are restless creatures. They buck and rear in the wind, constantly repositioning themselves, like sleepers troubled by Nightmare. If the Almighty watches from above, the Dunes must look like tiny worms wriggling just beneath the surface of a desiccated Earth. The superstitious tribes who move through these sands swear allegiance to Allah & to whatever mad deities were born in the land before the coming of their Prophet and linger still in the rocks and gullies. These people do not welcome the unknown. Since none has e'er seen a map, the Unknown is everything. Christians are the enemy. Other Arabs are also the enemy. It is complicated. It depends.

We muster each day at 4 a.m., & march till noon, when the sun grows too fierce to bear. We rest as best we can, given the conditions, then resume our Progress in the evening, as the Gen. commands. Water is the principal subject of concern. We carry what we can. The iron canteens we were issued at Alexandria have mostly been discarded in favor of goat skins purchased or obtained through barter from the Arabs. The taste is foul, but the skins are lighter, hold more fluid, and do not store up the heat as do the Cannonballs, as the men have dubbed the canteens. Priv. Stennett, our resident wit, suggests that perhaps instead of discarding them, we might fire them at the walls of Derna—if only we possessed a field piece!

Morale suffers, as perhaps it must in such a place. The grisly death of our Egyptian friend the Scarecrow has taken its toll, & the high spirits of the men have faded. We are mocked not only by the Arabs, but also the Greeks, who find our rituals baffling and comical. They are impudent fellows, shaggier than any men I've seen. Each sports a massive moustache and ringlets of long dark hair. They wear sashes and vests of scarlet and gold, & carry with them all manner of pistol, club, and dagger. They are greatly amused that only one of us—O'Dell—knows how to swim, and even he not well. Do we not customarily serve on ships? And what if the ship should founder? Then we'll sink to the bottom and march, says Mason—if that's what the Captain orders. This response occasioned outright hilarity. Obedience seems not to be a cardinal virtue among our Hellenic friends. I suspect they are better swimmers than soldiers.

MacLeish finds no humor in such jesting. He has marked two of the Greeks, and one of the Arabs, a one-eyed individual he calls the Cyclops, for a thrashing. I suspect he makes these threats idly, but the march has not helped his Temper. We suffer with the heat & thirst and paucity of air. Already I find my trousers want cinching. Mason complains of a galloping heart. He is senior man among us, and well acquainted with the rigors of the march. Yet he is also advanced in years, & shipboard they say was often in his cups. Near the end of our march this morning, his eyes rolled back in his head, & he gave an odd gasp, & toppled over in a dead Faint. Pvt. Moore was thereupon directed to take up the espontoon, and Mason was suffered to ride upon a camel. Stennett quickly voids whatever he eats, though he blames this on Dr. Rizzolo's too liberal administration of Rush's Pills, shell-sized tablets of calomel, jalap, and mercury. These pellets indeed exercise the bowels, but rather too vigorously it appears. He has trouble carrying his musket, much less his pack. Pvt. Moore and I help somewhat with this task, with my friend Prejean also willing to bear a hand. We are all gone brown and parched, like old bridles, and spend our hours covered in the infernal Dust.

Today we saw one of the Egyptians eat a Scorpion. He tore the stinger and claws from its body and wolfed the hideous thing down with only a sip of water. It is savory roasted, he said, but none of us cared to attempt this feat. In the mist of this carnival of Monstrosities we try always to remember the purpose of our journey, and to bear in mind the sufferings that must be the lot of our Countrymen, starving in the cellars of King Yusuf's prison fortress. We are coming for you, oh our Brothers. You are not forgotten!

* * *

All quiet tonight. The usual supper this evening of goat meat and porridge, though of lesser quality than when we set out on the march. We reckon we have covered about two hundred miles toward Derna, and a much larger number if one includes our detours and lateral movements across the harsh terrain, from desert to coast and back into desert again. No additional thefts.

10.

The Western Desert

Weston's army walks or rides, depending on the rank of its constituents, as the red god rises in pale streaks of light and then a deeper run of color like blood seeping up and spreading planewise at the horizon. The shadows of stones lie like pencil lines across the sand and the elongated shapes of men and their animals advance before them like leashes, pulling them into the darkness from which they have but lately escaped and into which they must return.

Gen. Malcolm Weston

Because there is little else to talk about as they march, the marines swap tales about their enemy. King Yusuf—"Yusuf the Usurper," as Weston calls him—is younger than his brother but a head taller, thick of neck and wrist and famously ill-tempered. He receives counsel from a blind woman who is described by some as heartbreakingly beautiful and by others as astonishingly ugly. She is said to be able to see into the hearts of the king's enemies. Yusuf keeps the sorceress in the Red Fortress—in a subterranean cell lined with iron, as metal is poison to her powers. She is escorted from this place under guard when the king has need of her visions. This need has increased of late. Yusuf sits on a throne made of human bones. He has built a machine of whirling blades that can cut a man into quarter-inch slices. He has a harem of twenty-four concubines, many of them

European, stolen from merchant ships in the Mediterranean and North Atlantic. He wears hoops of gold in his ears. He oils and perfumes his hair daily, and on feast days he drinks the blood of butchered Christians.

The air seems to tremble as heat rises up in waves from the yellow land. The particles of sand are clean and polished and catch the blaze of the sun like tiny diamonds in reflection so fierce that Sweet winces at the glare. He pulls his forage cap low over his brow and ties his kerchief around his face so that only a slit remains for his eyes. He has never been so thirsty. His lips have cracked and split, and his tongue has swollen to fill his mouth. Sweet knows that to sweat is dangerous. The prevailing wind blows from the interior. Under its treacherous caress his vitality is being sucked from him. He remembers what he has heard about the Western Desert. When, elsewhere in the Sahara, humidity is still at forty percent of saturation, it is only eighteen in Cyrenaica. Life here evaporates like a vapor. Dr. Rizzolo says that a man may go nineteen hours in this land without water. Thereafter he will grow confused, and wander without purpose. His body goes cold. The muscles of his legs cramp. He becomes dizzy, and can no longer recognize people or places. At last his eyes fill with light, and this marks the beginning of the end.

"Or the end of the beginning," says Colonel Ladendorf.

Dr. Rizzolo is a fussy, unimaginative man, the sort who feels facts are his personal property, not to be trifled with by others. He finds no humor in this remark. Sweet has to think about it. He is not sure Ladendorf made the remark in jest. The Dutchman is difficult to impress. Though his curiosity is boundless, his store of empathy seems limited. Occasionally when the colonel drops back to visit, MacLeish grows annoyed with his constant questions, and Sweet's stumbling attempts to answer them. MacLeish has found a number of reasons to resent his circumstances. He wants to know why it is, for example, that the *goddamned* United States Navy can't be bothered to transport this army of nitwits and nut-scratchers to its destination by sea, rather than forcing the *goddamned* marines to wear out their *goddamned* boot leather crossing this here *goddamned* desert. He is sick of the heat, of his thirst, of the dark skins and incomprehensible babbling of his supposed allies. He is particularly annoyed by the Dutchman, who seems indifferent to the conditions around him. Yet when the big man's irritation surfaces today, it is for some reason directed at his closest friend. When Sweet is asked to sing a favorite song, MacLeish pipes up instead, croaking the bloodiest verses of *Crawford's Defeat by the Indians.* Every schoolboy knows the story of Colonel Crawford's death at the hands of the Mingos. MacLeish is aware that the song bothers Sweet. The young man has airy notions regarding the essential goodness of humanity. In conversation he has gone so far as to speculate that such goodness might be shared by the redskins. He is troubled by the thought of torture. It does not fit with his vision of the future: the many nations of man, arms linked in amity, striding together into bright regions of Scientific Progress. So MacLeish sings out of spite.

Colonel Ladendorf takes no sides. He simply glances from one man to the other, his head inclined at an angle, as if he were making notes to himself.

"These Indians," he murmurs, caressing the words with his tongue. "They burned your countryman?"

"It's a fact," says MacLeish.

"While he yet drew breath?"

"Aye. And with one of our own looking on. A white man. Simon Girty. But they got what was comin' to 'em in the end."

"*Ach.* So yours is not such a civilized country after all."

"That was the olden days," says Sweet, his lips pinched in annoyance. "In Ohio. The Indians were riled by the scalping of their families by frontier militia. And that ain't even the right *tune.*"

Now MacLeish and the Dutchman join together in amusement at the young man's outburst. It seems to Sweet that their laughter is harsher than it needs to be.

11.

Sunlight and Shadow

The next day the Spaniard appears at the tail end of the column. Sr. Rivera wheezes. He limps. He has wrapped a stained bed sheet around his shoulders, and he shivers while others sweat. It hardly seems credible that he can walk the miles. And yet he does, at first in silence, occasionally glancing sidelong at the two Americans. Aside from his physical infirmities, it is clear he is uncomfortable in the company of the marines.

His voice, when it comes, is hoarse and difficult to hold in place. The words are a mix of Spanish and English, with a smattering of Latin thrown in and occasional phrases from half a dozen languages besides. There is little small talk. He feels he must tell them important facts about the *djinn. Genies,* he explains, in response to the puzzled expressions of the marines. *The Hidden.* Creatures of smokeless fire.

"And why would we give a tinker's dam about that sort of nonsense?" asks MacLeish. The only thing he hates more than a gentleman is a foreign gentleman.

"*Por favor,*" says the Spaniard. "Please. Indulge me. According to the holy book of the Mahometans, the *djinn* eat meat, bones, and the dung of animals. They live in communities and are ruled by *los reyes*—kings—fearsome beings of formidable powers. The *djinn* bring disaster and death. Although they can survive anywhere a flame can burn, in general they prefer remote and lonely places: deserts, crypts, *las montanas.* They occupy the gaps between shade and sunlight. They are active when darkness first comes. They also like marketplaces, and for this reason it is wise to avoid being the first to enter *el mercado* or the last to leave it."

The Spaniard is older, heavy-set, and mostly bald. Sweet supposes he is of peasant stock, as his hands and arms are thick and appear to have seen manual labor. But he is obviously educated, and he seems like the kind of man who is used to having an audience. Private Sweet nods as the Spaniard talks. He is vaguely embarrassed by what he hears. Nonetheless, he would write it down if he could. Not because he believes it, but because he is dutiful—and because he suspects that learning the legends of a people is almost as important in understanding them as knowing their language and marital customs.

Senor Rivera observes that Colonel Ladendorf often lingers with the camel train. His affinity for Sweet has been noticed. He tells stories, some say, as a way to stay close to his favorite. Sweet ignores the insinuation. Some *djinn* become attached to human beings, Rivera warns, and function like companion spirits. Indeed, the joining of humans and *djinn* in marriage is still practiced in some parts of the world. A mixed marriage is capable of producing offspring, though this is not desirable and can in fact be disastrous. The Queen of Sheba, who fascinated King Solomon, was part *djinn.* She is also said to have had one cloven hoof, like an animal, but this is not true.

"And what of Solomon himself?" asks the Spaniard, wiping sweat from his forehead and bushy eyebrows.

Sweet shrugs. "What of him?"

"It's said he built his great temple with the aid of the *djinn*—spirits of the air and earth, bound to his magical ring. *El anillo. Anulus.* They called it the...how is it said? The Seal of Solomon. It had power over all creatures, both mortal and eternal."

Sweet has not heard this story. He knows of the Good Samaritan. He is familiar with the Sermon on the Mount. Where he comes from, the Bible is an instruction book—a practical primer for those seeking salvation. Heaven is attainable. It has a sensible oaken door. One must work hard, seek a sound profit, refrain from unwise expenditures. One may then knock with a reasonable expectation of admission. And Solomon was a great king of the Hebrews, as he has recently been reminded. The son of David. Reverend Pool spoke of him from the pulpit one Sunday, as blue jays cawed outside. It was spring in Massachusetts, and Sweet found it hard to concentrate on the lesson. The church was so new that he could smell the sap in the beams. The private tries to think back, but can bring nothing about Solomon to mind. Instead he remembers how Jesus cast out the demons who had taken up residence in the men of Gadarenes. *Who are you?* Christ demanded of the squatters. *We are many,* the demons replied. What was the word? *Many?* No. *Legion. We are legion.* The demons asked the Lord to let them go from the men into the bodies of a herd of pigs nearby, and Jesus allowed it to be so. The animals then threw themselves into a lake and drowned. *A victory for Christ? Or for the undead?* Hard to say why the story has come to mind, or even what it means. Sweet has not thought of it in years. So many of the Bible's tales are embarrassing to a man of learning, as he aspires to be. An agent of logic and experience, not superstition. Yet it is hard for him to forget some of the yarns he's heard. His grandmother—his mother's mother—told dark fables about the woods west of the farm. Ghost stories, mostly, about evil redskins who walked with Old Scratch in life and who were bound to serve him in death, and pure but foolish maidens who strayed from the road to tarry with a handsome stranger. The maidens were never seen again, of course—though their panicked screams could occasionally be heard when the moon was full.

Sweet grins as he remembers the sounds of his grandmother mimicking the cries of these lost souls for her wide-eyed listeners—Sweet and his little sister, Clara, nestled together in bed. No matter how many stories she heard, Clara would always ask for more. Then, when the candles were put out and the fire died down, she'd tuck her head under Sweet's arm and listen to him breathe to help her go to sleep. The night seemed bigger then. It was a mansion of horrors: dark home to ghosts and fairies and things half-seen in the star light. But a child has a right to indulge in such nonsense. An adult has no excuse. Sweet has read Thomas Paine. He is familiar with the works of Buffon and Voltaire, though his French will not permit him to read them as he wishes. God exists, certainly: but as the author of immutable laws; a universal clockmaker—not the vengeful and capricious spirit of the Hebrews. Though he understands that vision of the Almighty better here. *No trees. No flowers. The heat.* Everything promising and delicate scraped from the landscape like flesh from bone. In the long miles before him Sweet sees thin columns of rock rising misshapen and bent like the fingers of some civilization buried whole beneath its ruins and the ruins of those who entered the land afterward. Spires, roofs, and temples swallowed. Languages crumbled to dust in the throats of those who spoke them. Earth stuffed in their mouths. They cannot scream. *Are the fingers reaching up, intending escape? Or are they extended to drag down through the blankets of stone and dust whatever they can reach?*

Senor Rivera's voice is as harsh as winter beside him. The stocky Spaniard says he has traveled with slavers who made their way through the southern waste to the *Bilad al-Sudan* and the green lands of Africa beyond. He has seen the rock ramparts of Idinen, Fortress of Ghosts, near the Wadi Tanezuft. Idinen is a mile high, crowned with a castle-like summit. According to the Berbers who live nearby, Idinen functions as a hall of council where the *djinn* meet to discuss their affairs. Pilgrims have reported hearing strange sounds on the mountain. Long, keening wails. Monotonous but hypnotic chants in a language that seems to run backward, like hymns to some incomprehensible pantheon. Occasionally human bones are found in lonely places on the slopes, and sometimes the bones are those of children, but the animals who live in this place refuse to touch these remains. Because of such happenings it is difficult, if not impossible, to get the locals even to look upon the oddly shaped rocks of the peak.

"But you have looked?"

"I have seen the Fortress of Ghosts," the Spaniard confirms. He trembles in the heat. His skin is pale beneath his sparse beard, and his lips are raw and bloody. His appearance suggests a mind that is drifting away from the truth.

"Are there...*djinn*? I mean, where you traveled?"

Rivera considers Sweet closely. There is something in his gaze that Sweet cannot quite pin down. Is it accusation, or an invitation? Even a madman is capable of nuance.

"My friend," says Rivera. "Open your eyes. The *djinn* are everywhere."

* * *

That night the heavens cloud up. Wind claws at the tents of the Christians, and thunder crashes like the fire of infernal artillery. The rain comes around midnight. Incessant. Pelting. By four bells the camp is inundated, and the ravines boil with run-off. All move to higher ground: man and beast, soldier and civilian. Tack and provisions are transported haphazardly. Around dawn the great storm moves north to vex the Mediterranean, with a few last clouds hurrying to catch it. Then the sun again. Steam rises from the sodden canvas of a hundred scattered tents. Corrigan, somehow pressed and neat, shouts commands at the men. O'Dell makes a troubling find. The rain has spoiled their remaining stores of Henderson's Veal Glue, a type of portable soup stored in wooden cases of thirty-six dehydrated slabs apiece. Certain of the marines find humor in this development. The soup has come from Newark and survived thousands of miles at sea. It is made of unidentifiable substances, and goes by the service name of Baked Vomit. It is viscous, tasteless, much reviled. But reliable. And now ruined by rain.

In the desert.

"Imbeciles," says the lieutenant. He is addressing Privates Stennett and Clay in particular. "Laugh while you're able. And learn to like the taste of sand."

This shuts them up. All except MacLeish.

"What was that, Private?"

"Not a word, sir."

MacLeish always has something to say. These days, it is often insolent. The emptiness of the region seems to embolden him. His resentment of authority seeps to the surface. Stephen Prejean eyes the big man with alarm. For all his japes, the cartoonist is a meek and dutiful soul. He is troubled by his unshaven comrade's grumbling. As soon as he can, he moves away. MacLeish watches him go—and spits at his heels.

* * *

It is Easter, by the western calendar. Hollis Mason suggests a holy service. As the old veteran is not notably religious, the marines suspect he is more interested in a break from the march than in commemorating the Resurrection. This is something they can respect, and they heartily second his suggestion. General Weston surveys his ruined camp and decides he is in no mood for hosannas. He orders an instructional reading instead. The Declaration of Independence. The Bill of Rights. The Egyptians listen respectfully, though only a few speak even a word of English. But the Greeks drift away. They have decided to roast two of their few remaining goats. They lay down their muskets. They are careful to keep them in sight.

12.

The Mahometan Yoke

Two hundred miles from Derna, the marines swap tales around the fire. It is widely agreed that Bonaparte is the Anti-Christ. How else to explain his rise to power—and his violent hostility to organized religion? Surely he has been assisted in his conquests by unholy forces. Some say he is preparing to invade England, and that his best troops will cross the Channel by hot-air balloon, suspended in wooden platforms beneath giant silk cannonballs launched from Calais. The balloons will drift on breezes deep into the shires. When they land, their crews will disembark to pull down churches, burn villages, and murder and rape the citizenry. An army of snail eaters traversing the globe on currents of air. It is enough to sober the thoughts of any English speaker. Can anyone slake the blood thirst of the French? America owes its independence partly to French assistance. And yet in the years since the Revolution, the U.S. and France—first a republic, now an empire–have fallen out. Following the Quasi War and the capture of the *Insurgent*, most Americans, including Sweet, now consider themselves firm allies of their former oppressor, Great Britain.

Weston brought a balloon of his own on the expedition, primarily for reconnaissance, but its basket was smashed in the storm. The marines are greatly relieved. None cared to tempt fate by taking to the sky in such a contraption. They've seen too much as it is. Every man here can recount tales of horrendous and legendary storms. Ships driven onto shoals and ripped apart by the surf. Schooners broken in two by monstrous waves, and all hands lost. Stennett and Clay have had enough of the sea. They would be content never to sail again. Prejean observes that this reluctance will make it difficult for Stennett to return to his wife in New Jersey. MacLeish volunteers to visit her in his stead, volunteering even to enter through the back door, if such is her pleasure. This offer brings only a few nervous laughs.

Repentance Moore changes the subject. As always, his mind is on the mechanics of mortality. He has heard tell that the pistol used to kill James Decatur in Tripoli Bay fired two slugs attached by steel wire. The wire wrapped around young Decatur's forehead, and the two slugs pierced his temples. The marines shake their heads. It is a fiendish weapon—more evidence of the perfidy of the Mahometans. Low mutterings ensue. All here are familiar with stories of white women captured by King Yusuf's pirates and sold into slavery. Defiled by the Moors—Purity Soiled—the leavings available even to their Nubian lackeys. And for Christian men no better a fate. Death in the galleys. Rowing in filth. Prisoners beaten on the soles of their feet until unable to walk. Colonel Ladendorf notes that King Yusuf's Christian slaves are subject to a variety of punishments. They are sometimes roasted alive in metal cages. At other times they are impaled, which is accomplished by placing the offender on the end of a sharp stake that is thrust up through the body until it appears above the shoulders. Slaves may also be cast over the walls of a town into a field of iron hooks. These implements catch the falling man by the arm pits, or the ribs, or some other part of the body, and slaves have been known to hang thus for several days, alive but in the most hideous torment. Crucifixion by nailing the hands and feet to a tree or wall is likewise practiced.

Two of the Greeks pause by the fireside to listen. One speaks rudimentary English. Together they communicate the sufferings of their homeland in bondage to the Ottoman Empire. In an annual process called the "harvest," one of every five boys is taken from rural communities, forced to convert, and sent to Constantinople to serve the Sultan. Most are never seen by their families again. It is worth a man's life to be found without a receipt for the *jizya*, the Sublime Porte's tax on all non-Muslim subjects. Periodically rumors spread that the Empire will force its Greek subjects to renounce Christ and take up the teachings of the Prophet. As a consequence, the people grow restless. There is fighting in the mountains. They say a man named Dionysius once led a revolt against Turkish rule. When he was caught, he was beaten, tortured, and then flayed alive. His skin was filled with hay, and this rude effigy paraded around the province of Thesprotia for the amusement of Turkish loyalists and the intimidation of those who dared to hope for liberty. And yet such atrocities have not dampened the Greek fervor for independence. Rather the opposite, it would seem.

The Greeks drift away, but the talking continues as the stars wander west. Will the marines find someone to fight? It is the question they all return to. And how will they acquit themselves if they do? Hollis Mason is no comfort. He says he has seen grown men cry in the face of a Shawnee charge. Cry, and worse. Call for their mothers. Turn tail and run. Or sit passively as the redskins hack the flesh of their scalps away from their skulls. *There's no recovery from that sort of shame,* says Private O'Dell. *Best to put a ball through your own brain if it should come to that. Don't you reckon, Sweetie?* But Sweet is no longer listening. He is thinking of home. He is hoping no rumor of cowardice on his part should ever reach his mother's ears. He has been unable to offer her material solace. He has accumulated no wealth, and does not seem likely to do so in the service of his country. But at least his mother has a notion of him as fine and young and courageous, and this itself is as good as gold. She said so herself. Lemuel Sweet is unwilling to see this vision tarnished.

Stennett offers a final observation. All he wants is for the expedition to scare all opposition out of Tripoli, so that no blood need be shed. Then the marines can quit this foreign foolishness and get back to fighting their natural enemy—the skulkers, thieves and ingrates of the United States Navy.

"Hear hear," says Mason. "To the Corps!"

"To the Corps," those gathered repeat.

It is sinking in. The marines are hundred of miles into the desert, surrounded by allies they don't trust and trudging forward to meet an enemy they are starting to dread. They have little to rely on but their muskets—and each other.

From the Diary of Lemuel Sweet, April 8, 1805

Little rest for me this night, & what little I have had was crowded with portent. We sit now in the frigid cold of the Desert before dawn. Yes—cold. When the sun sets here, the temp. drops rapidly. It is possible for a man to be sweating at the top of the hour and shivering by the end of it. It is another way in which the desert tries us. But I have precious little time for reflection. Soon the Lt. will appear from his tent, & gesture that he is ready for us to pack and stow his belongings & those of the Gen. We will assemble to break our fast with what little poor rations remain. And then the march will begin again, with many miles still to go.

For some reason I have been chosen as the recipient of cryptic communications from our Iberian gentleman. Sr. Rivera, who is often incommunicado due to his devotion to narcotizing Stimulants, and the inconvenient shortage of such substances on our Expedition, has seized on me as repository for a peculiar species of Delusion. He is convinced—and here I offer caution, as his English is worse than my Latin, and we struggle to communicate under the best of circumstances—that our translator and logistics officer, Colonel L, is of a different character of being altogether—a different Genus, to use the zoological term—than the men with whom he travels. I shall not use the words. They are clear enough, though suggestive of a realm of Phantasm and Superstition in which I do not care to traffic. Rivera is aware of the figure he cuts in our army, a figure rather of ridicule than of respect, & also of the indelicate nature of his Accusations. He admits that he acquired his English in Malta, while trying to quit his opium cravings. There he met and conversed daily with the poet S.T. Coleridge, who was sojourning in Valletta for the same purpose. He makes no excuses for his Infirmities. He asks only that I observe the Dutchman's personal habits for myself. Does he take victuals? Or drink? And if so, what—and when?

More later—called to Duty.

13.

The Ring

Weston sends word to Corrigan that he wishes to discuss tomorrow's march with Sheikh al-Tahib. Sweet is ordered in turn to fetch Colonel Ladendorf so that he may translate at their meeting. Sweet climbs to the nearest high ground, where he sees the Dutchman fifty yards to the west. The little man moves as he always does, his head swiveling from side to side as he takes in all around him, his feet leaving only the slightest impressions on the sand. He has dropped something. Sweet sees a flash of metal where it falls. He calls, but the Dutchman seems not to hear. The marine follows. In the dust lies a ring of purest gold, gleaming like the day it was made. Mounted on it is a blood-red ruby. It is the most astonishing thing Private Sweet has ever seen. Ladendorf walks on, apparently unaware of his loss, as Sweet surveys the scene around him. The camel drivers are arguing. An Egyptian soldier is climbing a promontory to the south. No one has noticed his find. The ring is his if he wants it. Into his britches— then hidden perhaps in the toe of his boot.

What is there to stop him?

He is briefly elated. Yet in the next instant he knows he cannot keep this prize. Never mind the words of the Spaniard. Sweet has started to feel it himself. There is something unsettling about the colonel. And thus too about his treasure, glittering in the sun. His quarry is now a hundred yards distant. Sweet forces himself to follow, and the Dutchman finally hears his cries. He turns and waits. Sweet places the ring in his open hand.

Ladendorf cocks his head.

"Pretty," he says. "Yes?"

Sweet shrugs. But his gaze is easy to read. It is the same look a hungry man has when he sees a table laden with food. The colonel smiles and walks on.

* * *

At dusk, two of Sheikh al-Tahib's men return to camp from a scouting expedition. They bring bad news. They have made contact with a group of Moroccan pilgrims heading east. The *hajis* report that when they passed through Derna, Governor Ali Rasmin had reestablished control of the city. It was also rumored that a company of King Yusuf's cavalry was just a few days away. They will certainly reach Derna before Weston's army, and thus be able to fortify it against the American advance. The camps boil with speculation. Colonel Ladendorf reports that there seems to be an agreement among Prince Ahmad's people and Sheikh al-Tahib's horsemen to return to Egypt. General Weston suspends all rations until the camel drivers promise to continue the march. A council is called. It is meant to proceed by fire light, but there is little to burn. Only the Christians show up. Disappointment is apparent on every face.

At midnight, Sheikh al-Tahib sends word from his camp. He has resolved to ride no further until he can confirm that the U.S. warships Weston promised are actually waiting for the expedition at the Bay of Bomba. To attack Derna otherwise would be madness. Weston's army is outnumbered, and may well face an entrenched foe. The sheikh agreed to fight fiercely. He did not agree to fight foolishly. His people advised him not to trust the Christians, he says—and perhaps they were right.

* * *

The next morning the sheikh gathers half the Arabs and makes as if to lead them back to Egypt. Prince Ahmad, wearing a shimmering purple robe and silver slippers, scurries over from his camp, followed by two of his aides, to consult with Weston. Ahmad worries that al-Tahib will not only quit the

American effort, but indeed that he will actively oppose it. He exhorts the general to do whatever is necessary to placate the Arab chieftain and encourage his return.

Weston listens impatiently. When he speaks, he speaks to all and none. "It seems to me," he starts, "that what is *necessary* is for me to tie the sheikh's heels to a saddle and have him dragged through the dust. Nothing will compel me to ask as a favor what I claim as a right. I would remind His Highness that the services of this desert raider are due and owing to the United States of America. I have paid for them, goddammit, and the sheikh has pledged to render them with fidelity. It is not his place to make terms or dictate measures." Weston spits at the silent sky. "I prefer an open enemy to a treacherous friend. Truly the Lord chose rightly between the sons of Abraham!"

A messenger is sent to the sheikh, charged with delivering just such language. The American general questions the courage of the desert race, and vows to publish this timidity in the markets of the western world. When the rider returns, he reports that Weston has touched a nerve. Al-Tahib is red with anger. He swears he will tolerate no further insults from Weston and his Crusader dogs. The general considers the messages with a smile. He orders a march, and the column gets underway at half past eight. Just after noon, a messenger from the sheikh arrives to report that he has changed his mind. *Sheikh al-Tahib will rejoin the expedition,* says the note, *if the prince will halt to await his return.* Prince Ahmad is agreeable, and spreads the word to his followers. Much to Weston's displeasure, the column stops, and temporary shelters are erected.

An hour and a half later, the sheikh canters into camp at the head of his men. The Greeks scramble for their muskets. There is much shouting as al-Tahib presents himself at Weston's marquee with three of his followers. Corrigan, Selim Comb, and Lako Androutsos hasten to join them. Standing sentry outside the general's tent, Sweet hears high words within.

Ladendorf is called on to convey their meaning. The sheikh speaks first. "You see now the influence I have among my people."

"Yes," says Weston. "And I see as well the disgraceful use you make of it."

It gets worse. The argument rages for almost an hour. Eventually the Dutchman is dismissed. It seems as if the general and the sheikh are discussing him. Sweet can make out little of the halting Arabic Weston utters. But he knows the sound of Ladendorf's name, and he can distinguish as well one word, uttered with incredulity several times by the general.

Djinn, Weston says.

And then, translating for himself: "The Hidden. Surely you're joking."

The only response is silence.

* * *

The marines sleep with bayonets fixed. Not on account of any supernatural enemy. On this march, there is reason enough to be wary of the men they call their allies.

14.

Commerce

Next day at noon they meet a slave caravan moving east along the pilgrim road. The slavers wear black turbans and blue veils, so that only their eyes are visible. They sit their camels in silence, and are careful to display the antique muskets and blunderbusses in their possession. One carries a halberd, a weapon not employed on western battlefields for over a century.

The slavers are tall, slender, and warlike in demeanor. Their skin is yellowish, like the Arabs, and their clothing consists of loose blue trousers and a narrow shirt of the same color, with wide sleeves they bring together and tie at the back of the neck, so that their arms are at liberty. At a distance the whorls of black cloth around their heads look like helmets. At their waists they wear a dark-colored belt or girdle, and some carry in their hands a lance, neatly worked, about five feet long. Above the left elbow, on the upper part of the arm, they wear their national badge, a thick black ring of horn or stone.

With these warriors travel half-breed overseers, brown-skinned, shirtless men on foot, their eyes rolling in apprehension as the two groups of travelers pass each other at a distance of only a few yards. Hemmed about by the riders and overseers walk the slaves: three-score men, women, and children, black as pitch and caked in dust, their legs and feet grotesquely swollen and by their enormous size forming a wretched contrast with their emaciated bodies. The Africans make no sound as they pass. Most of them are naked, with decorative scars marking their foreheads and cheeks. A few wear dirty garments around their loins, or spread across their backs and necks. The men are shackled at the ankles and wrists, while the women and children are left unbound so that they may carry bundles of firewood and baskets of dates. Also two enormous white objects. Sweet initially takes them for logs of some pale southland tree, but this is misperception. *Ivory*, someone says. *Elephant tusks.* The slaves scarcely look up to see the men who watch them: Prince Ahmad's army, torch bearers of liberty.

"Tuaregs," says Ladendorf, nodding at the mysterious riders. "The men go veiled, while the women do not."

"Why do they cover their faces? Are they criminals?"

"Not by their own lights. They wear the veil so evil spirits will not recognize them as they journey through the world. Some Tuaregs travel on their errands deep into the south, where the gods are vicious and insane. The amulets are protection. Always silver. Never gold. Silver signifies purity. Each carries the Koran in the pouch that hangs from his shoulder."

"Why are those two staring at you? Do you know these men?"

Ladendorf tilts his head, as if to eavesdrop on the distant conversation.

"They are superstitious. One claims to have seen me before."

"He's not happy about it."

"No. He wouldn't be."

Sweet shakes his head. "They're gonna kill them little ones."

"Fear not, Private. There's no profit in corpses. They'll stop to rest before they enter Alexandria. It is well known that the hair of the females should be arranged in nice order, and that their bodies should be oiled so they glisten. The men will be shaved to give them a good appearance. The children will be fed, and required to dance. African children are said to be jolly. Did you not know this?"

"They don't look so jolly."

"Ah, I had forgotten. You come from the brave new republic. Ignorance and unhappiness are unknown to you. Are there no slaves in your land?"

Sweet blushes. Ladendorf does not seem interested to hear his response. It is as if he knows the truth already.

"Indeed there are," Sweet calls after him. "We're called *marines.*"

But the colonel is not done with the slavers. Two of the half-breed overseers approach him, leading a girl of perhaps ten years. Mostly knees and elbows, the girl is terrified, and the overseers have to chivvy her along with harsh words and flicks of their leather crops. While they speak in a language none save the colonel can understand, it seems as if they are trying to give him the girl. Ladendorf is unmoved by the gesture. When the overseers attempt to insist, the colonel grows cross, and shouts at the Tuaregs who sit watching from their mounts some distance away. Finally one of the Tuaregs gestures to the overseers, who hurry the girl back toward the rest of the slaves. The Dutchman looks around and shrugs. The march continues.

"Hell," says MacLeish. "I'll take one, if they're givin' 'em away."

But Sweet is the only person who hears him.

* * *

That night, long after all the campfire banter has ceased, Sweet has a dream. In it he wanders through green, well-watered country, much like the Berkshires back home. Pastures have been cleared, and fat sheep pull at lush tufts of grass. He stops to exchange pleasantries with a bay mare that stands in a stone paddock. Her breath is warm on his neck. But as evening approaches, the private realizes he is lost. The path he is traveling ends in a tangle of vegetation and fallen fence posts. Sweet wanders further afield and his surroundings grow strange. Brown fields lay unattended by any save crows, great scabrous creatures that watch him without fear. Leafless trees stand stunted and twisted by the wind. He is in a region of empty creek beds and brittle gray briars.

At last he spies a house of stone and small windows that towers over the surrounding wilderness like the head of a camelopard over-topping the jungle foliage. Sweet knows better than to proceed, but he enters anyway, drawn by laughter that echoes in the halls and grows faint as he approaches. There are portraits on the walls, elaborately framed oil paintings either recently completed or untouched by age, so vivid are their colors. Though he doesn't recognize the faces, he finds them disturbing just the same. There is some emptiness in the expressions, a sense of finality in the features. Deep in the bowels of this structure, wreathed in shadow, Colonel Gustav Ladendorf sits at an enormous banquet table. Snakes coil and intertwine at his feet. Before him in an ornate bowl is a dark cold soup, and beside the bowl is the colonel's golden ring, lustrous even here in the gloom

The little Dutchman eats with a spoon, his tongue flicking out occasionally to catch some morsel on his lip or a corner of his mouth. Sweet is not offered a taste of this provender, but it's just as well. The young man is preoccupied. He has realized what is so peculiar about the portraits around him: all of the people in them are *dead*. Not alive when portrayed, and since deceased, but dead at the time they were painted. There is no laughter here. The air is still. Ladendorf stares at the marine standing in front of him and his gaze is neither welcoming nor dismissive and at length it is apparent the colonel is about to speak. Sweet dreads the words, though he cannot say why. He clenches every muscle in his body. The Dutchman opens his mouth and all goes black and Sweet sits up, fighting to free himself of the dream. The night air is cold. A man crouches over him. Sweet is vaguely aware that the man has been touching him. *Searching.* The figure places a finger to his lips.

"Beware the Dutchman," whispers Senor Rivera. His rank breath steams in the morning air. He says the words as if he has been practicing them. "He is a creature of great evil, and he wishes you ill."

In the middle distance, they hear a scream.

15.

The Dutchman

Confusion and excitement. Men running. Shouts. At first light the one-eyed man the marines call Cyclops is found dead just a few hundred yards from the American tents. The condition of the corpse is similar to that of the Scarecrow. The man's torso has been torn asunder, the lungs and liver partially consumed. There is little blood left in the body. Again speculation runs rampant. Though several men heard what they believe to have been the Arab's final cry, no one saw the struggle. One difference: with this killing comes evidence of theft as well. The dead man's distinctive dagger, a long poniard with a rhinoceros-horn handle, is missing. Find the weapon, says Sheikh al-Tahib, and you will find the killer. He turns his gaze toward the Christian camp. Surely there are some who take his meaning.

* * *

Malcolm Weston is in one of his declamatory moods. He is polishing his oratory. It is rumored that he will run for office when he returns to the States.

"Our army has now marched hundreds of miles through inhospitable terrain," he says, "without seeing the active habitation of any fellow creature, or any signs of organized commerce, save of course for the shameful traffic in Negro flesh. Still this multi-national coalition of liberators advances, availing itself on occasion of those sad worn paths where pious Mahometans walk or crawl toward Mecca." Weston rises to the topic. He cannot resist. He stands outside his tent and reads aloud. "Superstition has marked her lonely steps over burning sands and rocky mountains, whence the revelations of one of her fiercest fanatics has created for her wretched victims a tedious pilgrimage to pay their devotion at a distant shrine. But while we reproach the creed, we cannot but ascribe some good to the effect of its imposition, as it has here and there opened a water source to the Mahometans, which now allays the thirst of a sterner band of pilgrims, bound westward across this blasted waste in a quest vastly different from that which leads east to Mecca; namely, the liberation of three hundred Americans from the chains of Barbarism, and the institution of a manly and vigorous Peace."

"Sir," says MacLeish, who is standing sentry at the entrance to the tent.

"Well?"

"Well what, sir?"

"How does it sound?"

"A lovely poem," says MacLeish. Shuffling his feet. His face has turned an alarming shade of red. "The honest are always abused by the wicked."

The general sniffs as if the big man's words carry an unpleasant odor. "It's not a poem."

"Sir."

Weston addresses the other sentry. "You."

"Sir?"

"Sweet, yes?"

"Yessir. Lemuel Sweet."

"You are acquainted with Colonel Ladendorf, are you not?"

"I am."

"Step inside, if you would."

The general seats himself behind his traveling desk. It is dark inside, but no cooler. Two candles burn on the desk. Sweet pauses to get his bearings. The air smells of mildew and unwashed bodies.

"At your ease, private."

"Sir."

"That's enough *sirs*, thank you. I've known a few marines, mostly from back when you fellows wore green. Good men in a pinch. But how shall I say this? Not exactly the sort a gentleman would have as a dinner companion. You, on the other hand, seem to be cut from different cloth. I hear you have some schooling."

"Grammar, Latin, and Mathematics, along with a fair amount of Classical History and the Natural Sciences. I had hopes of university. At one time."

Weston opens one hand. *Continue,* it says.

"My father incurred a number of debts before he died. He speculated in the market for export of ginseng to the Orient. After he passed, we lost our farm, and his effects were sold at vendue. I had no trade. I needed to make my way in the world."

"Siblings? Could they not have contributed?"

"I have a sister. Clara. She is…deficient. Of little help to my mother."

"So you found yourself at market, am I right? And a friendly sergeant was kind enough to buy you a flagon?"

"There was beer involved. I was told it was small beer. The effects indicated otherwise."

Weston's laughter is a series of barks.

"No need to blush, son. I recruited for General Wayne when we fought the Miamis. Occasionally a man has to be convinced he has a taste for adventure. Tell me, what is our government paying its marines for their services these days?"

"Six dollars a month, sir."

Weston snorts. "A sailor can make three times as much."

"With experience, yes. And still not have enough to drink."

"Ha. You have the right of it there. Well, if it were up to me…"

"Thank you sir."

The general lowers his voice. He hoists a thumb at the entrance.

"How did you become involved with that great brute? MacLeish, right? And what happened to his ear?"

Sweet steps closer. "He lost it in a fight last summer. Lopped off by a cleaver, in a dockside tavern in Bristol. Defending me, if truth be told. And as for how we became mates, he was my first friend on the *Wasp*. He showed me the ropes, as they say."

"Looked after you, did he? That's admirable. A warship can be a treacherous place for a young man. You were hazed, I take it?"

"I was. Till Donald put a stop to it."

"Donald?"

"Private MacLeish, sir."

"Ah. Well, I won't tell you your business, Sweet. But I will suggest that it does not enhance your prospects for advancement to fraternize with individuals of low breeding. That's all I'll say on the subject. And indeed, it has nothing to do with why I summoned you. I have come to trust our Colonel Ladendorf. He has a familiarity with the customs and geography of the region that would be difficult, if not impossible, to replace. He knows every language spoken in these parts, and he has done just as good a job—maybe better—at communicating with the various contingents that make up our army as his unfortunate predecessor. You remember Mr. Karam?"

"The men called him Scarecrow. He was a pleasant sort."

"So he was. Pleasant indeed. His death still troubles me—as does the murder of the Sheikh's man last night. The corpses violated like that. I haven't seen the like since my days at Fort Reliance. Wolves will do that to a body, you know. Pieces everywhere." Weston's voice trails off. He grunts to himself before he refocuses on his audience. "We were lucky to find so able a replacement for Mr. Karam as the colonel. He can read the night sky like a surveyor's map, and he knows where to find water better than the natives do."

Sweet is silent.

"And yet. How do I say this? I've had the most confounding letter from the British consul. Or…no, that's not quite right. That sounds like it just arrived. We're too far west for dispatches from Alexandria at this point. This came in on the fourth day of our march. I found it just yesterday, stuck to the back of sealed correspondence from the fleet, forwarded by Sir John." Weston brandishes the paper. "Before I start. Lieutenant Corrigan tells me that you and your friend out there were at least partly responsible for bringing Colonel Ladendorf into the expedition in the first place. Is that so?"

"It is, sir. We found him…happened upon him, really. In Alexandria. He was being attacked."

"Attacked?"

"By the gypos. A group of them were beating him with sticks."

"I remember now. Extraordinary. Did they say why?"

"Why, sir?"

"Yes, private. *Why.* Why they were beating Colonel Ladendorf with sticks. It seems like an obvious question."

"I'm sure they did, sir, but it was in the local tongue, so we had no way of knowing."

"And he wasn't hurt? He seems sound enough."

"As best I can tell, the colonel suffered no injury at all. They did seem very angry with him, though. I reckon they meant to kill him. Private MacLeish persuaded them to stop."

"Private, you do yourself credit by sticking up for your messmate, but I have no doubt of Private Macleish's methods of persuasion. He's a great ox of a man, isn't he? Another Peter Francisco. At any rate—the letter." The general flattens the dispatch on his desk and leans forward to read it, his forehead just a few inches from the page. "No help from the Turks. I expected as much. The Turks have troubles of their own. Their empire is being torn to pieces. Russians to the north. The Serbs in the Balkans. The Greeks—Good God, the Greeks—it's only a matter of time. But Sir John tells me he has identified our Colonel Ladendorf, about whom I enquired before departing Alexandria. The colonel is a man of considerable learning. We could see that for ourselves. Well versed in the European traditions of military science. An intrepid explorer. Fluent in several tongues, *et cetera, et cetera.*"

Weston takes a sip of water from the pewter cup on his desk. Sweet watches, impressed. He had almost forgotten there were such things. If the general were to pass him this vessel, the private is unsure whether he would drink from it or try to leap into it.

Col. Gustav Ladendorf

"Only one matter of concern," says Weston. "A Swiss engineer named Gustav Ladendorf accompanied a French expedition into southern Abyssinia some years ago. The group was trying to get to the equator—one of three concurrent geodetic expeditions sent out by Louis XV to gauge the circumference of the earth. The other groups went to Lapland and South America. Quite a fascinating endeavor. The African expedition was unsuccessful, I'm sorry to say. It was attacked by bandits and thwarted in its mission. Four French geologists—one a member of the *Academie*—died. Our Dutchman disappeared, presumably slain as well, though no witnesses attested to such."

"He seems well now."

"Indeed he does. In splendid health. He goes days without food or drink, with no apparent ill effect."

Sweet nods, relieved.

"Perhaps he was lost in the desert for a period of time."

"Perhaps he was. A good long time."

"Sir?"

"This expedition I mentioned."

"Attacked by bandits?"

"Indeed. Attacked and overwhelmed. In April of 1735."

"I don't understand."

"Nor do I, son. It's probably a mistake. And yet... Colonel Ladendorf is not an ordinary man, is he?"

"I would agree with that statement."

"It's possible he's not what he seems. I suspect the Grand Sultan is not sure what to make of our mission. Whoever rules Tripoli is supposed to kowtow to Constantinople. Prince Ahmad's father was a loyal vassal of the Ottoman Empire when he ruled Tripoli. His brother is most definitely not. Yusuf has been ordered by the Sultan to cease his piratical activities on at least three occasions, and yet he persists. So perhaps we are doing the Turks a favor by deposing the usurper. On the other hand, we are armed foreigners on imperial soil, and we, as Americans, spread the bright promise of liberty. Our friend the colonel—if he *is* a colonel—might be along as the eyes and ears of the Empire."

"A spy, sir? Isn't he a bit old for that?"

"You misunderstand me, Private. It can't possibly be the same man. Our Dutchman is evidently an imposter. To what purpose I know not. Do you think you could keep a weather eye on Colonel Ladendorf for me?"

"You mean...?"

"Exactly. Let me know if you see anything out of the ordinary."

"I can do that. Indeed, you're not the first to ask."

"No? Who else?"

"Senor Rivera, sir."

"Good Lord. The Spaniard?"

"He is obviously unwell. I did not agree to the request."

"How odd. The one man I most regret putting on the rolls in the first place, inquiring about the man who has done me the best service. Perhaps the Spaniard thinks Ladendorf hid his laudanum. If he did, he should be rewarded for it. Shameful, that habit. It will make a wretch of the strongest soul. Did you know that, Sweet?"

"I have heard it. I'm surprised Senor Rivera has made it this far."

"As am I. Surprised, and maybe a little disappointed. He's a gloomy bastard. Seems to travel with a black cloud over his head. Bad influence on morale. I wish I had a beer to offer you, son."

"To remind me, sir?" says Sweet.

"Eh? Remind you of what?"

"Of my taste for adventure."

"Adventure. Oh, aye." But the general is no longer wholly present. His big head swivels so that Weston's eyes appear to be focused on a spot just over Sweet's right shoulder. If the general is looking into the future, he does not seem to be encouraged by what he sees.

"Well, whether you've a taste for it or no, you'll get your share. Sir John begged me to call off the expedition. He said we couldn't possibly succeed. But at this point we have no choice, you see? We've gone too far. A counter-march would be ridiculous. I should look a fool to posterity. The nation's honor will not permit it, and nor will mine. I don't know what sort of man Colonel Ladendorf is, or why he is assisting us. He upsets the Arabs, I know that. They say he's…well, never mind what they say. And the colonel himself seems unimpressed with the higher ambitions of our mission—the inculcation of a democratic spirit in the peoples of this land. Nevertheless, he does assist, and I will make use of him. I have to. We are going to capture the city of Derna. We will seize Derna, rally the populace of this region, and proceed west to take Benghazi. Then we shall march on Tripoli to rescue our countrymen. We will go down in history as liberators, Private. Or we shall surely die in the sand."

From the Diary of Lemuel Sweet,
April 17, 1805

Perhaps it is the nature of the desert to act as a sort of furnace or foundry of Character. The men around me grow harder. The General in particular. He rarely circulates in camp anymore. He rides apart. He plans. He talks to himself, principally about his chief concerns, water and time. Water is a constant worry, and our progress suffers for the detours we must make in pursuit of it. This means delay of course, and Stennett says the General feels every hour wasted threatens to keep us from our rendezvous with the vessels of the Navy that are meant to meet us at the Bay of Bomba, and support our approach to Derna. So set is the General on his goal to invest this easternmost city of Tripoli that not even the gentlemen dare to question either his moods or his methods. He imagines himself on a Stage, with all the world his audience. He is a captive of his own announced Intentions. He must move forward.

The Sheikh who leads our Arab horsemen is similarly disposed, though with different motivations. He grows more difficult by the day, and resentful of any check or restraint. He is a disputatious sort, whose features seem to be set in a perpetual scowl. Though he professes support for the aims of the Mission, it is said that he does so for reasons of his own. The Colonel reports that the Sheikh and his clansmen are disciples of an especially dour brand of Mahometanism, one that brooks no dissent or departure from the words of the Koran. They come not to liberate Derna but to scourge it, as it is said that some among the populace have spurned the true Faith in favor of alterations proposed by King Yusuf and his minions. The General may speak of the virtues of democratic rule and self-governance. I observe that the Sheikh listens to this talk with difficulty. His plans for the city involve rather more bullets than ballots. And considerable unhappiness.

The last of the dogs has disappeared. Worm Bait, most called him, tho I preferred Jack. He was a loyal soul, and I had grown fond of turning to see him following the column at a respectful distance. I suspect one of the camel drivers did away with him. They have no love for dumb creatures, and to them an animal of low breeding is worth nothing save contempt.

Only porridge for sup this evening, with a lump of rancid butter.

Sentry outside the Genl's tent.

Cold again. And the troublesome dreams continue. Though I continue to be the recipient of the Colonel's visits at the rear of the column, I confess I would rather be shed of him. The Spaniard is no better. Always he eyes me with suspicion and what I believe to be malice, though he persists in trying to warn me of some vague menace posed by the Dutchman. Unfortunately, he is unable or unwilling to tell me more specifically what the danger is. Nor can I make him. A private in the U.S. Marines has his freedoms stripped from him upon enlistment and occasionally returned to him as rewards, piece-meal, if his commanding officer's temperament permits. I have no ability to compel either the Colonel or Senor Rivera to turn their attentions elsewhere. I know it is irrational, but I feel at times that I am like a strip of disputed territory in wartime, contended over by rival armies, destined to be ruined by the conflict.

16.

Citizens of the Desert

The air is still this morning as the marines march into an expanse of dunes, mountains of earth tortured by the wind and rolling northwest for miles downhill to where the Mediterranean shimmers gray-blue in the false distance of the heat. By half-past ten the expedition is climbing a crumbling bluff of glassy sand mixed with shingle, dotted with tamarind and thorn bushes. In the afternoon they arrive at a vast plain bordering the sea, called in Arabic *Oak korar ke barre.* Two tribes of the Bedouin people have gathered here, over a thousand souls, covering a territory of twenty leagues' circumference. They live in clusters of black tents, sharing the ground with vast herds of sheep and goats.

Weston's army contains the first Christians ever seen by these people. According to Colonel Ladendorf, the Americans in particular are viewed with astonishment, fair-haired curiosities from some wild-eyed *fakir's* show that has traveled worlds and contains within it representatives of all that is terrifying and comical about the unbelieving lands beyond the *ummah wahida.* The marines enjoy the attention. Old Hollis Mason, balding and irascible, takes out his false teeth and chases a gaggle of shrieking children, snapping the wooden chompers open and shut like castanets. O'Dell shows off his tattoos, a lurid gallery of mermaids and daggers and burning skulls. Even MacLeish joins in. The big man is persuaded to load four sheep on his shoulders—two on each side—and makes a great show of striding to and fro about the camp, followed by several idolatrous boys.

There is much discussion among the Arabs about hats. Only Christians wear them. Old men laugh at the oddity of the Greek and American uniforms, but gaze with open lust upon the

Westerners' hastily polished muskets and bayonets. At the same time the tribesmen observe the greatest deference toward those of the foreigners who bear any distinctive marks of office. They bring for sale everything their camps afford, and as rarities offer up ostriches and young gazelles. Being destitute of cash, the enlisted men can only pledge rice and biscuits in exchange. This lessens the Americans' stature somewhat in the eyes of the tribesmen, but dignity is restored when it turns out the Bedouin will accept the marines' brass buttons in lieu of currency. The tribesmen think the metal of the buttons to be some rare alloy, and marvel that Allah should allow unbelievers to possess such wealth.

Sensing a receptive audience, Weston orders a demonstration of the Girandoni air rifle. Private O'Dell advances to stand in front of several dozen spectators. Pausing only to point the weapon skyward after every shot, so as to activate the automatic loading mechanism, he fires twelve rounds in rapid succession at a number of pre-placed targets. The rifle is not especially accurate, but it spits out projectiles at an astonishing rate. Young boys shriek with delight. Their fathers regard each other gravely. Weston has on previous occasions felt compelled to explain that the firearm is of Austrian manufacture, and has many practical limitations. Its air reservoirs, for example, are extremely difficult to manufacture, and subject to leak and rupture. The marines have a total of ten, each of which is good for approximately thirty rounds. But now is not the time for qualifications. This display of firepower has boosted American prestige.

The marines eat dates of an excellent quality, brought on a journey of some five days from an oasis in the country's interior. It is good to have the fruit, as the column's provisions have grown scarce. Fortunately, the tribesmen are fond of rice. A woman offers her daughter to Lefebvre, the long-haired Frenchman, for a sack of it. The girl is a comely brunette of thirteen years, well proportioned, with expressive hazel eyes and gleaming teeth. Lefebvre adjudges the transaction fair, and the girl does not object. Weston is known to be prudish in these matters, so Lefebvre is not eager to publicize the arrangement. Also, it is unclear how he came by the rice. MacLeish was in charge of the commissary, and later he takes his turn with the girl. It is his favorite topic of conversation thereafter. He did not mean to hurt her, he says. It is unclear whether anyone believes him. But bruises heal quickly enough, and the girl is seen in camp the next day. It is not until the following morning that Sweet finds the body.

The young private is walking the American perimeter an hour before dawn when he spies what he at first believes to be a dog, loping away from him up the slope of a hillside fifty yards distant. Or...not a *dog*. There is something odd about its gait. It looks like an insect. In the darkness Sweet thinks it could be a spider, so strange and stiff are the creature's movements, but the figure is too large. Sweet stands and surveys the terrain, trying to re-order his senses. He had previously been contemplating the peculiarities of the ostrich. Its two-toed feet, and remarkable speed. The wings—apparently useless, though prominent—and peculiar copulatory organ, unique among avians. Such thoughts now vanish. Just in front of him lies what he takes to be a piece of tent cloth. As he steps closer, though, he is forced to revise his assessment. It is the Bedouin girl. Her chest and stomach have been ripped open and her interior portions gleam in the moonlight. Pieces of her heart lie nearby like the petals of some dark flower. Beside the corpse lies the girl's head, her glassy eyes wide with fright and disbelief.

It is worse than the Scarecrow.

It is the worst thing he has ever seen.

A shepherd sees Sweet running to report his find. The Bedouin investigates, and word of the slaying soon spreads. Others hurry to the scene. A minor riot ensues, as the natives demand punishment for whoever is responsible for the girl's murder. Private Sweet himself is accused, though he is able to show that his skin and uniform are free of any blood or signs of violence, and is thus acquitted in General Weston's mind.

Later that morning, as preparations are made to bury the child, a group of men is elected to speak for the tribes. Many grievances are brought forth. Addressing these representatives through Colonel Ladendorf, Weston consents to take evidence regarding the identity of the killer. When none is produced, he points out that the author of the crime is unknown, and not necessarily a constituent of Prince Ahmad's army. He neglects to mention the recent fatalities of his translator and of the sheikh's man, the Cyclops. This logic proves fruitless. The girl's mother is brought forward, dramatically bereft, and a demand for monetary compensation is made, which Weston summarily refuses. The tribesmen thereupon refuse to trade any further, and go so far as to cancel a deal for the sale of forty goats Weston was counting on to feed his men. By afternoon the tension is palpable. Sheikh al-Tahib listens to the complaints and plainly sympathizes with the tribesmen. But he says there is little he can do. He orders his men to leave the Bedouin camp before nightfall. As the cries for vengeance grow louder, the general too orders his men to resume the march. It is a hurried departure, much to be regretted. Weston had hoped to recruit allies from among these wild people. No chance of this now. Two tents are left behind, along with a quantity of rice and several dozen goatskins of water.

The army is shadowed deep into the night by a hundred men of the tribes, on horse and camel. It looks as if bloodshed will come earlier than planned. But the pursuers eventually despair of attacking the technologically superior expedition, with its diabolical repeating rifle. They fade back into the dust, heaving shouts and curses at the marines and their allies. The Greeks shout back. They came to fight. One group of Arabs will do as well as the next.

"Such a shame," says Ladendorf, glancing back along the trail they have traveled. "She was a beautiful thing."

"Thing?" says Sweet.

"You know what I mean," the colonel explains. "The girl."

17.

The Temptation of Lemuel Sweet

Two nights later, raiders sneak into camp and steal five of Prince Ahmad's best horses. Weston sends out a detachment in pursuit: three Arabs and three Greeks, led by Selim Comb. The men return two hours later. They followed the tracks of the animals, which were accompanied by a number of other hoof prints, presumably belonging to the horses of the thieves. The trail heads south. The general suspects vengeful tribesmen from the encampment by the sea are behind the crime. They have fled into the desert, he says, in order to disguise their identity and true destination. The Miamis employed similar tactics in Ohio. Eventually the thieves will have to veer northeast to return home. Selim Comb's detachment is reinforced, and heads back toward the Bedouin camp to intercept the raiders.

☆ ☆ ☆

After six hours of marching, the army comes to a well twenty feet deep, at the bottom of which stands a pool of muddy water. The horses have not drunk since the previous day. When the marines with much difficulty procure a little fetid water, half the column presses near the well, Christians and Mahometans crowding each other for a chance to drink. In the struggle Dr. Rizzolo's pack horse is forced forward from the group. The animal slips and plunges into the well with a medical bag and two cloaks draped across her back. She snaps her forelegs in the fall. One of the Greeks pulls a pistol, but Corrigan stops him. The lieutenant tells Repentance Moore to fetch the Dickert rifle instead. A sniper's weapon, the Dickert fires a forty-caliber ball

from a forty-eight inch barrel scored to guide the ball in flight.
Moore loads it deliberately, with close attention to the charge.
Like Daniel Boone, who once shot a British officer through
the forehead at two hundred yards, he is careful always to use
the same amount of powder. The Virginian is slender and soft-
spoken, but there is an emptiness in his expression that inspires
caution in his companions. They sense that killing is of no more
moment to the man than his daily ablutions. The mare screams
and thrashes in the shallow pool below them until Moore puts
a ball through her left eye. The shot is greeted with a murmur
of appreciation. Even the Arabs take notice. Say what you will
about the armies of the world: none boasts finer marksmen
than the Americans.

The soldiers pull as much water as they can from the pool
and drink it, blood and all. Corrigan has one of the camel
drivers' boys lowered by ropes to retrieve the medical bag
and cloaks. The mare is left where she fell, as there is no
practical way to remove her.

* * *

When Weston calls a halt to the march that afternoon,
the expedition is within a few hundred yards of the ocean.
The general walks with Sweet and Dr. Rizzolo to the shore.
Here a handsome bay is formed by a spit of land that extends
into the Mediterranean a league and a half, terminating in
a high cape. The Arabs call the inlet *Salaum*, though the
promontory is marked on Weston's coastal chart as Cape
Luco. Notes on the chart say that the bay has served in
the past as a shelter for Maltese merchant ships. Weston
estimates they are ninety miles from the Bay of Bomba.

Selim Comb and his trackers return to camp to report
that they were fired at in the hills. They have lost the
stolen horses and the thieves who took them. The tracks
bend southeast, into the sand sea. It is a haunted region,
says Comb. To follow would be madness. But Prince
Ahmad grows frantic. The horses represent a significant
portion of his fortune, and he is anxious to have them
back. Corrigan sends Sweet to find Colonel Ladendorf.

Perhaps he knows where the raiders are heading. *Toward the Tibbo of Burgoo? Or the Kingdom of Fezzan?* But Ladendorf is always elsewhere. Sometimes it seems like he can only be found when he is not actively sought. An hour later, Sweet catches a glimpse of the man some distance to the west. It takes longer to reach the colonel than he expects. Ladendorf is always slightly ahead of him: just beyond a gulley; heading into a small space between the rocks. Sweet would shout, but the air is dry, and he cannot make the words. The two figures progress through a shallow valley littered with hunks of murky green glass and then up the flank of a barren hill. Halfway to the summit stand the ruins of three stone columns, mute and forgotten. The marine drinks the last few drops of water from his goat skin. Sweat stings his eyes. Climbing again. Sweet knows he will be late returning to the expedition. Indeed, he is *already* late—but he cannot seem to stop.

Ladendorf moves effortlessly, but Sweet is breathless by the time he catches up. The colonel stands at the mouth of a small cave and together the men survey the terrain they have traveled. It is a vision of desolation. Distant mountains, brown and gray, tremble in the heat. Sweet has until recently thought darkness to be the refuge of all that is unholy. So it was in Massachusetts: the forests dim and airless, the paths between the trees difficult to distinguish even at noon. But here nighttime is a sort of solace. Daylight brings the horrors: the thirst and fatigue and terrible glare, too bright to keep an object in focus. Things here move and flit in his peripheral vision, visual rumors appearing and gone in an instant. *Is this hell?* he wonders. *Not some vague analogous condition of temporary discomfort but hell itself? And the sun the face of a vengeful god?* It is an odd, unwelcome thought. He has forgotten for the moment that there is no hell, and that God is neither vengeful nor benevolent. *The Universal Clockmaker,* Sweet reminds himself. *The Supreme Intelligence.*

"Beautiful," says Ladendorf. "Yes?"

In the distance they see the dust raised by the army. Sweet notices that the column is moving away from them. He wipes his forehead with a sleeve of his jacket. "I'll be glad to see the back of it, Colonel."

"Ah. But you will never see the back of it. In some corner of your mind you will know it is here. All this emptiness."

"The general requires your assistance, sir."

"Doesn't he always?"

"The missing horses. Did you not hear me call?"

"I heard you. I chose not to attend."

"I meant no disrespect. Only—"

"Only you're following orders. I understand. You have happily surrendered the free will men speak of so warmly. And all for a few dollars a month. Is that what a man is worth these days?"

Somehow they are now standing inside the cave. Sweet wonders if the heat has affected him. He feels dizzy.

"What shall I tell the general, sir?"

"Yes. What shall you tell him? What *can* you tell him?"

Sweet knows better than to answer. The conversation has veered off course and a chasm yawns in front of him. It is difficult to see in the darkness, but something is down there. Something inhuman, and spiteful. "I'm not sure what you want me to say."

"What I want, you've already given."

"Joining the expedition?"

Ladendorf shrugs. He removes his spectacles and places them in a pocket of his waistcoat. "I see no expedition. I see bags of blood and bone crossing the rock. First one way, then the other. Year after year. Centuries. A carnival. Building and breaking."

"Why are you helping us, then?"

"I lead you on a fool's mission. As all missions of this sort are. Is that help?"

"The army is…?"

"All your armies."

"My armies?"

"Yours. Yes."

"Why are you telling me this? Why not the general? Are you in league with the Turks?"

"The *Turks*. Surely you understand by now. Of course I'm in league with the Turks. I'm in league with all of you. I help any army I can find. I guide the Romans. I arm the Jews. I watched Hossan slice Queen Dhabba's pretty head from her shoulders and send it to the Caliph. I build the tower and I tear it down. I watch men kill each other and I encourage them at their work. It is an old habit. The general is an idiot."

Sweet is silent. The Dutchman's sudden shifts of temperament are confusing. He is amiable one moment and enraged the next, for no apparent reason.

"I brought you here for a reason, my young friend. A gift."

"I don't need gifts."

The ring again. In the palm of his hand. Sweet has thought of it several times since he first saw it lying in the sand. The gold is heavy and incorruptible, as lustrous now as the day it was dug up. And it holds a ruby the size of a raspberry. A stone of immense value. Enough to buy a farm back home. Enough to buy *two* farms, and men to work them. Colonel Ladendorf gazes at Sweet as if he has just given the young man a great prize.

"Don't be hasty, Private. Try it on."

"As I said, sir, I don't need it."

"Maybe not. But your sister could find use for such a thing, yes? Little Clara? She is simple, you say. Can find no situation, and thus is of no help to your mother."

Sweet shakes his head. "Surely that is none of your concern. What do you want?"

"Ah," says Ladendorf. He closes his hand around the gift and takes it back. "But that is the wrong question. The question is, what do *you* want? Has anyone ever asked you that, Private? Your officers, for example? Has anyone considered for even an instant what would make you happy? You don't care about gold. I can see that. Too complicated. Making decisions for yourself might be a bit too much for a young man of your capacity. And clearly you don't care about helping your family at home. But they can take care of themselves, after all. Perhaps it's the fairer sex that interests you. Yes? Your lower regions grow heavy at times, do they not? Heavy because they're *full*. Because you carry seed within you, hot and thick and imperative. I can give you a girl whose touch will bring you more joy than the embraces of a thousand mortal women. A girl whose breasts sit firm and cool in your hands. Whose private places taste like sugar, and smell like honey, and fit around you like a wet warm glove. That would please you, I think. I can show you places you never dreamed exist. Cool places, shrouded in the mist of water cascading off rock. Will you come with me, Sweet? When the expedition is over?"

"Come with you? Where?"

"I have errands to run. Many places to see."

"Why would you want me?"

The colonel's mouth spreads in a lover's smile, indulgent and somehow condescending as well. He places a hand on Sweet's cheek. "Because you are difficult to obtain."

The private takes a step back. "But for what purpose? I don't understand."

"I need a country. Flesh and feet. The one I travel in is wearing out."

Sweet glances at his companion. Not at the stained linen blouse or the faded red kerchief he wears but at Ladendorf's face. His *hands*. The older man's palms seem to wrinkle and darken as if scorched. Ladendorf removes his stained hat. His hair is a wiry fringe of orange around his head. Scabs have formed on the peeling scalp. Ladendorf grins, and his teeth have disappeared. He is ancient now. *Hideous*. Sweet realizes he can smell the Dutchman. It is no longer the smell of old coins. It is the odor of carrion. The stench of rotting flesh. A fly crawls out of one corner of the colonel's mouth.

"Good Lord. What *are* you?"

"The Spaniard hasn't told you? Between his fits of lunacy and craving?"

"He's told me a lot of things. Not all of them make sense. He said that you are not what you seem to be. I don't know what he—"

The Dutchman sucks air over his parched lips. Congeniality falters on his face and something darker appears instead. A grimace. A sneer. His whisper becomes a hiss.

"Did he tell you he wants you to take him from *behind*, like a horse?"

The colonel's eyes glow like embers fanned by a breeze. In the still air, the sound of Sweet's breathing seems immense.

He can hear his own heartbeat. He feels the air growing heavier, as if the world is about to fall in on him.

"Surely you know what the priest is after, Private. He wants you to keep him warm at night, and listen to his simpering, and tell him his sins will be forgiven because you are an evil young thing in need of redemption and he is the only one who can help you find it."

"He said I should watch you, Colonel."

"You're not a god seeker, are you? A knee bender? An ass kisser? I thought you were smarter than that. You know he's *lying*, your God. He says you're something, but we both know it's not true. You haven't a dollar to call your own. Your mother's living on hand-outs and poor little Clara will be alone in the world soon enough. Perhaps she'll go to the ports and sell herself for bread. Lemuel Sweet's fetching young sister. Fucked in the mouth for a half-dime a toss. You're nothing, Private. And you've done nothing and *will do* nothing and…"

"He said—"

"—one day a hundred years from now a pilgrim will find your skull in the dirt and kick it aside because you never existed at all."

"He said to *watch* you. And that if I watched, you would reveal your true nature. And so you have."

The voice now. Crooked and coarse, like a ruined saw blade.

"My nature is nothing you'll ever understand, you brainless shit. I was here before you pewling apes came crawling out of the forest and I'll be here when the last of you are nothing but dust. You disappoint me. I thought you were smarter. But suit yourself. There are plenty of others who want what I can give them. You'll make a better fit with my friends below. An entire army swallowed up by the sand, and desperate for a drink. Go with your God, my young soldier. And see how little it helps."

Ladendorf holds the private's gaze with his own. There is sunlight in his eyes, and fire, a flame so bright and hot that suddenly Sweet's head swells with pain and he sees nothing at all. The world around him goes blank and silent and the single sensation available to him is the pulse of

blood in his eardrums. Next he becomes aware of the
frantic staccato thump of his heart. He hears a whisper,
very faint, from nearby. And another. Something touches
him. Sweet blinks and tries to focus. The glare fades. He is
still in the cave. A sharp object—a stick, perhaps—scrapes
the back of his neck. He moves sideward, but stumbles over
what looks like a skeletal shrub. Something is in his hair. It
yanks at his collar as if to reach for his throat and it is not
one thing, but several. Several sticks. Or bones. A dozen. A
hundred, insistent and inescapable, jabbing at him like the
pinpricks of insect legs, like spiders or centipedes crawling
over his skin. Sweet's arms jerk wildly, reflexively, and he
tries to scream but the effort scrapes his throat like a knife.
He can see men reaching for him from the walls and floor
and ceiling of the cavern: soldiers in ancient metal, their
faces pitted and gray, their mouths gasping for air. Thin
tufts of hair hang from their foreheads, and their tiny eyes
sit deep in the sockets of their skulls. They are pulling
themselves out of the earth. The thought flashes through
Sweet's mind that this is the lost army of Cambyses, the
doomed Persian soldiers buried alive by weather or
witchcraft thousands of year ago and unseen since by any
who lived to tell. He cannot say for sure. Nor does he care.
He knows only that they want him. He can sense it. *A new
recruit.* They will march in tired lines through long halls of
twilight and they will end up here in this dark dry place,
upside-down in the dirt, an army of the dead dreaming
forever of rivers and the rustle of wind through green grass.
Dreaming of something to drink. Any fluid will do: sweat;
tears; spit; blood. They will take it just as the desert takes
it, take the last warm drop of marrow or mucus and suck
it up into their own rough ragged mouths. Sweet thrashes
as he fights the hands that are attempting to take him.
The faces are everywhere, jeering horrid masks of hunger
as colorless as driftwood and making some sound that is
either anguish or appetite. There is a moment when the
young man's strength has reached its limit and he feels he
cannot escape the fingers that tear at his neck and his hair
and his ankles. The shrunken lungs of the dirt soldiers hiss
and shriek at him and he gags on the smell of death in the

air but there is a sliver of light ahead of him, a tiny aperture that seems to be growing smaller, and he lunges toward it, snapping with his boots and elbows the brittle bones and teeth of the creatures that are trying to hold him back. And then somehow he is free—free and falling, tumbling down the dunes, still screaming and striking out at invisible hands.

✳ ✳ ✳

When he stands it is because the sand is burning his back. He has no choice. He is dazed and alone and he is walking again. Walking and weeping. He has no memory of how he got to where he is. All that happens afterward is unclear, a dream as puzzling as the shimmering horizon itself, changing aspect from one step to the next. He knows he will die here. He wonders if he already *has.* Not literally, perhaps, but for all practical purposes. He composes plaintive speeches in his head. Eulogies for his childhood. THE CASE FOR ADVENTURE. Certainly. MAKING ONE'S WAY IN THE WORLD. *But what if the world betrays you?* What if the world takes you by your soft young hand and leads you to the strange last stanza of a poem you never knew you were writing: a lad of Massachusetts, alone in the Western Desert, attacked by the unholy in a land empty of everything but the dead and decomposed?

Naturally Sweet is fair and sober-minded in contemplating his own downfall. At Least He Tried. But at the edge of his brain sits an editor, crow-like and cross-eyed, who rewrites his prose. The Promise That Was Sweet, says the golden boy. FAIR-HAIRED AND LIVELY. *Indeed—though unable to master even the simplest trade.* THE FAVORITE CHILD. *Of course. And little Clara without a thought in her head. What kind of a contest is that?* A BRIGHT FUTURE IN FRONT OF HIM. *But not a dollar to his name. He died without knowing a woman. Laughed at by History—if History notices at all. Author of a thousand feeble daydreams.*

So why not lie down? His fate has been written. It is the heat that kills his spirit. It is thirst that murders his mind, despair that does the rest. He mourns for his mother and sister. The colonel was right. No good has come of his existence. No help to anyone—not even himself. He is lost in low valleys. He sobs. He sings. The sun stands directly overhead, as it does in this land, and there is no shade. He is hot and then cold and then hot again, and he is speaking but not to anyone near. And the light: growing brighter.

Invading his eyes.

Melting his head.

He has lost his hat and coat but it isn't enough. He tears off his shirt. His boots. His trousers. It is no relief. He wants to bury his face in the dirt. Perhaps it is cooler there. He could enlist in the sightless gray army that sleeps beneath his feet. Perhaps he could hide with them for a minute, out of sight of the sun. *Dig.* The crust is hot, but beneath the sand and rock is a place where the sky will not plague him. If he digs down deep enough...

But the end is not unpleasant.

Someone speaks. The words are strange and guttural but he recognizes the language as an antique form of English. Someone is holding his hand. He thinks for a moment that it must be his mother, but this woman has auburn hair that spills from her bent head to tickle Sweet's cheek and throat. Life returns to him: down the gullet. Into his belly. This is what salvation feels like. Creek water falling over rocks. Ferns on the bank of a stream, and the shade of a hundred trees. The faces hovering over him are framed by white cowls. Their eyes are metal blue and ocean gray, and their foreheads are inked with Latin words: *Poena. Absolvere. Redimere.* Questions. They are asking him questions. Sweet answers as best he can. He has never been interrogated by a dream. Or perhaps not a dream. Perhaps they are ghosts. Or *angels.* Do angels exist? He hasn't thought so for years.

How did he come to this place? ask the faces. *What is his errand in these regions?* Sweet is naked. The air moving over him smells of mint and rain and he is content to lie where he is. *Zerzura,* he thinks. *I have found you.*

Still the questions come. The men in the cowls say they are looking for a thief. An evil being, old beyond reckoning, that cannot create but can only tear down. A malicious spirit that always wants what it cannot have. The creature they seek has stolen from them an object they would fain recover. It is a pretty thing, this object. It is a ring of purest gold, adorned with a ruby.

Has he seen such a thing?

Sweet smiles. He knows this answer, and is happy to tell it.

* * *

Another voice, now. Not so comforting.

"Why do you make this?"

"What?"

"Why do you make this face, English?"

"Not English," says Sweet. "American."

"You are a fool. And blessed, as fools sometimes are."

"Where am I?"

Still the sun. Bright now. *Hot.* But tolerable. Sweet opens his eyes. There in front of him, sitting on a black gelding, is Selim Comb. He is a formidable man, with a massive moustache and a clean-shaven head the size of an anvil. His lips move as if he is talking to himself in some long and uninterruptable monologue. One of the Greeks is beside him. Translating.

"You are found," says the Greek. "That's all that matters. Two days are we looking."

"Where are they?" says Sweet.

"Who?"

"The people who…tended me."

The Greek says a few words in Turkish. Selim Comb squints as he scans the horizon. He exchanges glances with the Greek before he responds. Another one of the riders dismounts and offers Sweet his goatskin. The water is rancid—nothing like the fluid he received from the hands of the red-haired woman. He drinks it anyway. He is unable to refuse.

"No tenders here," says the Greek. "No people for many miles."

Selim Comb speaks again.

"Only ghosts," adds the Greek. "But one question."

Sweet nods.

"Who killed these men?"

Sweet is baffled. "What—?"

He looks around. The ground behind him is littered with corpses, battered and bloody, their eyes wide in agony.

Their faces are painted red and their heads are bare on one side, long-haired on the other. A dozen horses stand with their heads down in the midst of the carnage, as if they are ashamed of what they've seen. Among them are Prince Ahmad's Arabians.

* * *

Sweet is unconscious when they bring him in from the desert. The marines laugh themselves to distraction at the sight of their naked comrade. He is sunburnt and scratched and scabbed in a dozen places, but he is alive, a miraculous find in a land seemingly empty of even the slightest good luck. Sweet is not the hardest worker among them. He is neither the fiercest nor the most competent of the group. But he is good-natured, and a willing hand, and he indulges their visions of themselves. They are fond of the youngster, and they had feared the worst.

Lieutenant Corrigan, on the other hand, acts as if Sweet's return was a foregone conclusion. He has the young private jostled awake, and proceeds to berate him for costing the expedition valuable time. If it happens again, Sweet will face corporal punishment. The lieutenant has brought the cat o' nine tails along for just such an occasion. As it is, the unfortunate young man will be fetching water for his comrades until they reach Derna—and possibly beyond.

Sweet is wrapped in a blanket and escorted to General Weston's tent, where he attempts to explain how he was found surrounded by Prince Ahmad's horses and six dead bandits. Given water and cheese, he revives enough to understand the question, but has no answers to offer.

"I was lost," he says.

"After you left the colonel?"

"After the colonel left me."

"Yes. Well, the colonel returned to the column, as he was supposed to. But these men—these *bandits*. When did you meet up with them? And what in God's name happened to the poor bastards?"

"I don't know, sir. I thought I was dead."

"You may be yet, if Lieutenant Corrigan has anything to say about it. You remember nothing?"

"I'm sorry, sir."

"No, no. Don't apologize, son. I believe you." Weston leans back in his chair and rests his hands on his belly. "Mr. Comb says the bandits were of a tribe called the Maxyes. Southerners. They claim to be descended from the warriors of Troy, though I suppose that's neither here nor there, for our purposes. Could they have fallen out, I wonder? And set upon themselves?"

Sweet shakes his head. "I couldn't say, sir."

"This isn't the end of the matter, Private. But I won't tax you any further this evening. You're a very lucky young fellow. See if you can get your comrades to help you to the doctor's tent. You'll need something for those burns. You look rather like a Maine lobster. And for God's sake—Mister Corrigan? If you please." The lieutenant appears as if he'd been expecting the call. "For God's sake, find some trousers for this man. And light duty only for the next two days. I'm afraid Mr. Sweet is not looking at all fit for combat."

* * *

Colonel Ladendorf has advised anyone who cared to listen that he was worried sick by the young private's disappearance. He has no idea how to explain it. Sweet had announced an intention to rest a moment before returning to the duties of camp, but the Dutchman never imagined the youngster could get himself lost while still so close to the expedition. Even so, he seems unexcited to see the private's return. Indeed, Prejean later comments that the Dutchman cursed upon hearing the news that Sweet had been found alive. For the moment, Sweet is too tired to care. His face and lips are badly burnt. He sleeps for fourteen hours. No dreams tonight: only the wind off the desert, and its murmuring complaint.

18.

Mutiny

Weston rides out at dawn, accompanied only by Colonel Ladendorf, who travels as always on foot. The two men return at ten. The general then leads the column three miles southwest and calls a halt near a pool of good water at the bottom of a deep ravine. The ravine has been carved from the rock by torrents of water and small stones that rush down the mountain during the desert's rare rains. The rift is invisible from fifty yards away, and shows no evidence of previous visits. Ladendorf has found water again, where neither Arab nor westerner believed it to exist. The feat is much remarked upon. No one can explain it. Sweet holds his tongue, as any remark he makes on this subject will sound like an accusation. Indeed he knows he can say very little about Ladendorf. Accusations of any nature against a senior officer are a dangerous business. More so here, when the accusation makes so little sense. MacLeish asks his friend what the hell happened in the desert, but Sweet shrugs him off. He resolves to tend to his own affairs, keep his mouth shut, and stay as far away from the colonel as he can. He suspects he will have problems enough of his own to keep him busy. Holding his head together. Trying to sleep without seeing the gray faces of the long-dead soldiers who tore at his skin and his hair. He thinks again of the Dutchman. Of that sly, insinuating smile, and the stinking flesh peeling away from his skull...

Yes. He will stay away. But will it be enough? Will the visions fade—or are they his, now, to keep?

* * *

Weston is ready to resume the march.

Prince Ahmad, on the other hand, asks that his pavilion remain in place. Weston demands his reason. When Ahmad answers that his horses require additional rest, the general's face goes red, and a vein appears at his right temple. Eventually he learns that Ahmad's real intention is to stay where he is until a scout returns, which he has already sent toward the Bay of Bomba, seeking news of the warships promised the expedition by the U.S. Navy. An audit is conducted. The army has three days' supply of rice, no bread or meat, and no small rations. Weston urges this circumstance as reason enough for the march to continue—and with greater haste. But the prince and Sheikh al-Tahib make common cause. They announce that they will proceed no further until their men have had a chance to recover their health and spirits, and to obtain news from the west bearing on the likely success of their mission. Weston tells them it is their choice, famine or fatigue, and orders all rations stopped. The Mahometans spend the afternoon in confusion. At a little past five p.m. the prince, harangued by his Arab supporters, strikes his tent, orders his baggage packed, and takes up a march toward the east. Weston and Lieutenant Corrigan watch impassively, not choosing to betray a concern for themselves or the prospects of the expedition. However, upon hearing from Ladendorf of a plan among the Arabs to seize the army's remaining provisions, Corrigan orders the Egyptian drummer to beat to arms. The Christians form a line in front of the magazine tent: Greeks on the right, marines in the center, Egyptians holding the left. Each party stands in opposition to the other for the space of an hour. A parley is conducted. After considerable argument on both sides, the prince decides to remain. Al-Tahib's Arabs reluctantly agree. Ahmad's tent is pitched again.

Thinking the danger is over, Corrigan orders the marines to conduct the manual exercise, according to their daily practice. In an instant the Arabs re-draw their weapons. Prince Ahmad mounts and puts himself at their head, apparently sharing their alarm. It is a remarkable sight: a clear snap at the hand that feeds. "The fat cunt," says MacLeish. "He dies first."

"Silence!" snaps Corrigan. "I'll tell you who to kill."

The tribesmen spur forward at a trot, shouting the words of the Prophet. The marines stand motionless as the enemy approaches. Sheikh al-Tahib points out the Christian officers—Weston, Androutsos, Selim Comb—and cries out in his shrill dialect.

Weston nods at Corrigan.

"Present... *arms!*" says the lieutenant.

The muskets move in unison. The marines are not men; they are parts of a mechanical implement, gear teeth on a giant flywheel, unmoved by the prospect of the death they are about to deliver. Uniform movement startles the Arabs. Some of the prince's followers exclaim and curse. One, in English: "For God's sake, do not fire! The Christians are our friends!"

Senor Rivera stands with the marines. The Spaniard is unsteady on his feet, but his sword is drawn. Lako Androutsos and his Greeks remain steadfast. Some of the others are agitated. One of the Egyptians abandons the line, but Corrigan is unfazed.

"Private Moore," he says. "On my command, put a ball through the brain of our friend the sheikh."

"Aye, sir."

Weston steps forward and strides toward the prince. As he advances, he warns Ahmad against committing a desperate act. A clamor drowns out Weston's voice. Ahmad is distracted. At this critical moment, three of the prince's bodyguards ride between the two men, brandishing scimitars. Weston ignores them. He threads through their horses to get to Ahmad, and words pass between them in French, a language few here understand. The prince glowers at Sheikh al-Tahib, who deems it wise to quit the field. Weston turns and walks back toward the marines, relief apparent on his face.

"There will be no mutiny today," he announces.

* * *

An hour later, the sheikh appears at Weston's tent. He brings two men with him. They are obviously frightened. A dozen more Arabs follow, several with weapons in hand.

Colonel Ladendorf explains. "The sheikh says these are the men responsible for the earlier misunderstanding. They spread false rumors. They said the Christians were planning to kill the prince, and that General Weston intended to offer up the Arabs to Governor Ali in Derna as captives. It was these rumors that upset Prince Ahmad. The sheikh brings the culprits to you for punishment. He bids me to tell you also that these men indicated that *I* was the source of the rumors." Here Ladendorf pauses. He cocks his head, listening patiently to the sheikh. "He adds that I am instructed to tell you I am not what I seem, and that I am no longer permitted to visit the Arab camp. On pain of death."

Ladendorf poses a question to the sheikh in Arabic. The sheikh spits in response.

"*Immediate* death," Ladendorf adds.

Weston sighs. He holds out his hands, palms up.

"Tell the sheikh I have no quarrel with these men. I require obedience from his forces, but they are his to command as he sees fit."

Ladendorf starts to translate, but the sheikh interrupts. It is obvious he has no patience for the Dutchman; indeed, that he dislikes even the sight of him. He calls for his sword, a scimitar with a blade almost three feet long. A puddle of piss forms at the feet of one of the captives. Weston says a few words in Arabic, but the sheikh is no longer listening. The men are made to kneel. The sheikh steps up beside the first. He raises his blade over his head, holding it with both hands. Sun flashes from the metal when he brings it down. Sweet hears a swish and a kind of chopping *thud,* like a cleaver going through beef, and the condemned man's head seems to jump off his shoulders. The head hits the ground in front of the kneeling figure and rolls from side to side. The heart continues to pump for a few seconds, and at each beat there is another gout of blood. Sweet sees the dead man's hands open and close spasmodically three times before the young marine turns away from the sight. He closes his eyes during the second execution, which requires several strokes. Again there is considerable blood, but it disappears quickly. The desert is thirsty. Somewhere under this scorched land is a *reservoir* of blood. A vast sunken sea of it. Ladendorf watches from a few feet away. He glances at Sweet, and smiles.

The sheikh speaks again. He is pointing at Private MacLeish.

"Good God," says the general. "What now?"

Ladendorf translates. "He says the private killed one of his men. The big one, who had the use of only one eye. Rashid by name. Your men called him Cyclops."

"And he thinks *MacLeish* did it? What is this accusation based on? Anything?"

"He says you can check the private's tent, and there you will find the dagger owned by Mr. Rashid. It is a distinctive weapon, with a handle fashioned from the horn of a rhinoceros."

Weston summons MacLeish.

"Is this true, Private?"

"Is what true, sir?"

"Did you kill the Arab?"

"Which Arab?"

"Have you killed *any* Arab, Mr. MacLeish?

The big man grins. "No sir. Not yet."

"Do you have property that belonged to a man of the sheikh's contingent?"

MacLeish may not have been listening before, but he is starting to understand. "What property?"

"Just answer the question, Private."

"A portion of tobacco, sir. That weren't being properly attended to."

"I'm not talking about tobacco. Is there anything else?"

"Not a thing, sir."

Weston nods to Corrigan. "Go."

The lieutenant returns two minutes later. He holds the poniard, which he reports he found with MacLeish's belongings—exactly where the sheikh said it would be. The officers inspect the object as if it could tell the story itself. The weapon looks lethal and outlandish, and all the more valuable for its sudden notoriety. Argument ensues. The Arabs take the dagger as undeniable evidence that MacLeish is a murderer. Under their code, his life is forfeit. Weston is not so easily persuaded. He asks the sheikh how he knew where the poniard might be. The Arab responds that he was given the information by one of his men. Weston asks which one. The sheikh indicates the second of the two headless bodies that are even now being dragged off toward the desert, trailing twin signatures of gore. The general exchanges glances with his officers. The Arabs are waiting. He knows he has to do something. But in the common law, possession of stolen property is by no means proof of homicide—and besides, he cannot afford to lose another marine, much less one as fearsome as MacLeish.

In the end the matter is settled to no one's satisfaction. Weston reports that under the customs of his country, a man may not be sentenced to death for murder without the testimony of at least one witness to the crime. The general cannot deny, however, that Private MacLeish appears to be in possession of stolen chattel, which is a separate and clearly punishable offense. Therefore the man will receive the discipline commonly accorded the crime of theft, a number of lashes to be determined by his commanding officer. This is not quite right. Under American naval law, a captain has limited discretion in this regard; he can order no more than twelve lashes on his own authority. A greater number can only be assessed by a court martial. But there is no time for such niceties. The Arabs grow restless. Weston knows he must act, and act quickly, if he is to hold the expedition together. Forty strokes seems about right. It won't kill the big fellow, but it will probably leave him unconscious, and doubtless create an impressive mess.

Corrigan produces the white baize bag. Every ship has such a bag, and every sailor and marine knows what it contains. Weston nods, and the lieutenant unwraps the cat o' nine tails. It is a wicked little flail, composed of a two-foot-long leather handle and nine lengths of cord, each a foot and a half in length. MacLeish stares in disbelief as he is stripped of his jacket. He looks to his fellow marines, and his gaze lingers on Sweet. But Sweet is confused. Events are moving too fast. For a moment he'd thought his friend was to be hanged. This lesser sentence is a reprieve, harsh though it may be.

Next comes the linen blouse. MacLeish's back is much remarked upon, covered as it is with waxy scars from a previous flogging.

"Sir," he says, "this ain't *right*. I didn't take no bloody knife. I never touched it."

The lieutenant answers.

"Belay that, private. The decision has been made."

"What bloody decision? It's a *lie*, goddammit. They're all goddamned *liars!* Heathen liars!"

"Private, shut your mouth. Or I'll have you gagged."

As MacLeish will not consent to let a Mahometan administer the beating, and no marine will agree to do it, a Greek is chosen instead. There is nothing to tie him to, so the luckless private's hands are bound before him and he is ordered to kneel. All gather to watch, forming a ring several men deep. The scene reminds Sweet of a cock fight he saw in Madeira, save that here the onlookers are silent. MacLeish endures the flogging without a word, staring straight ahead, biting down hard on the strip of harness leather he has been given by Selim Comb. The Greek is a stout man who has apparently done such work before. Donald MacLeish's shoulders are quickly rendered a bloody mess, with strips of skin and hair hanging like some gruesome fur from his back. Only as the last lashes descend do tears fall from MacLeish's eyes, and trace lines like a tiny map in the grime that covers his chest. His comrades look on sympathetically, but he will not meet their gaze. When the punishment is over, Sweet rushes to his friend's side. Dr. Rizzolo is close behind. Sweet places a hand on MacLeish's head. MacLeish opens his eyes and after a moment focuses on the younger man. Sweet is unsure what to say.

"The honest," he offers, "are always abused by the wicked."

MacLeish's massive fists, still bound, catch Sweet on the temple. Even this glancing blow blurs Sweet's vision. But it is the most the big man can do. MacLeish collapses face-first in the dirt, leaving the doctor in peace to tend to the bloody flesh of his back.

19.

Deliverance

Three days after the executions, hunger and fatigue retard the march. Weston orders one of the camels butchered, and exchanges another with the Arabs for their last two goats, which together provide a measure of relief to the Christians. There is water and some scant vegetation for the horses, but the expedition's provisions are essentially gone. The men are without

sheikh al-Talib

bread and salt. The next morning Arabs and Christians alike scatter across the plain in search of roots and grass. A species of wild fennel grows in low patches in the ravines. It is bitter, but it gives respite from the cramps that plague them. Sweet's lips are cracked, and he has trouble forming words. Even his new jacket seems heavy. He can barely support it. The Greeks suggest eating some of the horses, but Weston will not hear of it.

"Might as well eat the ammunition," he says.

* * *

Next day they arrive at the Bay of Bomba. It is a disappointing milestone. There is no fresh water here, and nothing to eat. More importantly: no American warships.

Ladendorf questions an Arab shepherd who states that he observed two vessels in the bay some days earlier. But the ships are gone, and speculation holds that the Navy has left the coast because Weston missed the rendezvous date. It is entirely possible. The expedition is eleven days late. But it is also possible that the ships will be back. For the sheikh, however, this is the last straw. Nothing can persuade him to believe that any Americans have ever visited these waters, or that there is a chance they will return. Al-Tahib calls Weston and his men imposters and infidels, and says they have drawn the people of the desert into this situation with treacherous views. All begin to think of the means of individual safety. Weston recommends a last push to get to Derna, but this is dismissed as impractical. *Without the support of naval gunfire,* asks Prince Ahmad, *what will we be able to accomplish once we get there?* The Arabs resolve to separate from the army the next morning. The general leads the Christians to a bivouac a quarter-mile away, and orders that fires be maintained on a promontory to the rear of their position.

It seems clear that matters must soon come to a head. There is commotion in the Arab camps for much of the night. Messengers dash back and forth between the prince's retinue and the sheikh's contingent, and muskets are fired as men argue themselves into readiness for slaughter. But at eight the next morning, at the instant when the various contingents of the army are about to set at each other's throats, an Egyptian ascends the bluff for a last lookout. There he discovers a sail.

All rush to survey the sea.

"Fury," Corrigan announces—though in truth the ship, hull down, is little more at this distance than a pinprick of white. *U.S.S. Fury* is a schooner-rigged brig. She carries only eight guns. But she sails as consort to the *Endeavor,* one of America's splendid new frigates. *Endeavor* has thirty-six guns—twenty-four of them eighteen-pounders. She is capable of reducing the stoutest fortress to rubble in under a week. The sail grows larger. Corrigan is right. It is *Fury.* Cheers erupt from all assembled. Mason picks Prejean up in a bear hug and leads him in a jubilant waltz. O'Dell sings Irish anthems at the top of his lungs, and even the Dutchman is seen to do a triumphant jig, his yellow eyes alive with excitement.

* * *

General Weston is collected by *Fury*'s launch late that afternoon. The camp in the meantime moves around the bay to place itself in proximity to a spring of chalky but tolerable water discovered by Colonel Ladendorf. As the sun falls red in the west, provisions are delivered to the expedition by rowboat: hardtack, beef, a quantity of limes and cheeses. Weston remains on the brig all night. It is said the ship's commander admits to doubt that any white man would ever see Weston or his marines again. Weston feigns confidence. Or maybe actually feels it. But it is noted that he drinks the captain's Madeira with special gusto this evening, and that his hands have developed a tremor.

* * *

The marines occupy this ground for three days, eating and sleeping and taking from *Fury* the provisions they need to support their advance on Derna. Along with the food come gifts with which to win the hearts of the vanquished. Washington has sent three hundred and fifty tri-cornered hats for distribution to the natives. Manufactured in the city of Trenton, they are of excellent design, and only slightly out of style back home. It is surmised that the triangular bill will offer increased protection from the glare of the sun, thus providing the Arabs with a benefit they seem to have been unable to figure out for themselves. The tars have sent a partially filled firkin of rum as well, and Privates Mason and Clay get paralytically drunk as quickly as they can.

The day the march resumes is unexpectedly cool, marked by winds from the north and a fitful rain. The expedition travels ten miles over rocky country and camps in a shallow ravine, within a mile of a natural source of water that springs from the base of a mountain of freestone. They are approaching cultivated fields. A herald rides slowly through the Arab camp, reciting verses from the Koran as a warning to those who march under Prince Ahmad's banner. The herald visits the Christian camp as well. Rizzolo translates: *The punishment of those who wage war against God and His Messenger, and strive with might and main for mischief through the land, is execution, or crucifixion, or the cutting off of hands and feet from opposite sides, or exile from the land; that is their disgrace in this world, and a heavy punishment is theirs in the Hereafter! Be careful to destroy nothing. Let no one touch the growing crops! He who transgresses this injunction shall lose his right hand!*

Two days later the army makes its way over broken ground that is covered with vegetation and massive red cedars. It is the first semblance of forest they have seen during a march of forty-six days and over five hundred miles. For the Americans it is a welcome sight, and blessedly reminiscent of home. Their pace quickens. Every man feels the proximity of the enemy. It is an emptiness in the gut, a lightness in the head. They pitch their tents near a creek bordered with delicate blue flowers, five hours' march from Derna. The water is sweet and plentiful, and fields of barley surround them. But the men's sense of well-being is short-lived. A scout confirms the bad news. Ali Rasmin controls the city and is determined to defend it. Also, a Tripolitan brigade, sent out by King Yusuf for the defense of the province, has recently arrived in Derna. Alarm and consternation again seize the Arabs, and despondency the prince. They spend the evening in secret consultation. No Christian is invited.

Sweet stands watch outside the general's tent. In the great and profound darkness he sees the sky streaked with so many trailing sparks that it seems to him a great gale must be blowing through the outer heavens. *What does it mean?* he wonders. Perhaps the streaks are pen strokes of some vast celestial hieroglyphics—the Almighty's attempt to send a message to His Creation. If he could stand here for eternity and study the strokes, the import would become clear. Sweet knows he is but a small piece of an immeasurable whole. The desert proclaims it. And Africa, hiding behind the hills like fate itself, is huge and immoveable. Yet the Bible says God speaks to man. And he is a man, so he listens. But in the end the night sneaks off without a word, all promises of enlightenment undelivered.

In the distance, Sweet sees a tiny figure standing on a hilltop, silhouetted against the night sky. It is Colonel Ladendorf. *Watching.* As always. The private knows better than to wander far from where his comrades sleep. He suspects he is of no use anymore to the Dutchman. He might, indeed, be a liability. He is probably lucky to be alive. He scolds himself for his irrational preoccupations. Bible stories. God talking to man. And worst of all this gnawing unease at the sight of a small and aging officer standing a hundred yards distant. Whatever happened to him in the desert, Sweet reflects, it could not have been just as it seemed. *A man burning through his own skin. An army of the dead clawing out of the dirt.* Delusions. Insanity. The work of a fugue state brought on by heat and exhaustion. Surely this accounts for most of it. And yet though he can argue himself out of the most vivid of his recollections, he cannot wish away the lump in his stomach, or the sweat that worms its way down his chest and his back. He cannot get rid of his fear. A chill wind blows in off the desert, and when Sweet looks again, Ladendorf has disappeared. The young marine feels for the trigger of his musket. He whirls when he hears a footstep behind him, but it is only Senor Rivera. The Spaniard stands looking at him for almost a minute. At last, as if he has convinced himself of some important fact, he raises his right hand and makes the sign of the cross.

"Please," he says. "We talk."

From the Diary of Lemuel Sweet,
April 26, 1805

If these private musings shall ever come into the hands of another, I hope my Reader will undertake to understand the reasons I have made this record. I do not believe my senses to be disordered. I have suffered in the heat, as have my fellows, and I am much fatigued, but I am still in possession of my Faculties. I merely report what was relayed to me by Sr. Alfonse Rivera. I should say <u>Padre</u> Rivera, as he has disclosed to me that he is in fact a priest, dispatched by the man he and others of his faith call the Holy Father, with two other clergymen some months ago as a deputation to the Egyptian church in Alexandria.

Colonel Ladendorf, he says, is not human. It is difficult to express what the priest believes him to be instead; our ability to communicate is sorely constricted. I know only that Rivera fears and loathes the Dutchman, & that these feelings seem to be reciprocated. Of course the Dutchman is now widely disliked. The General continues to make use of him—indeed, the General relies on him, in matters great & small—but other than Weston he has no allies save perhaps my friend MacLeish, who has come to be the subject of the man's attentions the way I was initially. I would worry more on this point, but MacLeish is by nature immune to flattery and cozening, being an incorrigible hater of rank and privilege.

I have spoken with the General. He listens patiently, but in the end is unwilling to do anything to verify my allegations. He says the priest has come to see him as well, warning him against taking counsel from the Colonel. And yet the Colonel has given good service to the expedition by finding water along the route, & bringing intelligence of unrest among the Mahometans. General Weston knows that the Dutchman is unpopular. It is my belief that he suspects more than this. But while the expedition has need of assistance in this land, Ladendorf will be allowed to provide it. The General offers vague assurances that once we have taken Derna, and during any time we spend in the city, he will assign a man to monitor the Colonel's doings. In the meantime, he warns me not to believe everything the priest cares to say.

I know the stories about the Papists: the Midnight Orgies, the sacrifice of children and Nuns in their secret ceremonies. We in New England are aware that the French Catholics of Quebec would like nothing more than to expand their borders at Yankee expense. I have accordingly been wary in my dealings with the priest, not only because of his creed but also on account of his physical Infirmities, which are well known to the expedition. He says—I know of no reason not to be plain anymore—we are in grave danger. The Spaniard glances about him as if to make sure we are alone. Then he leans close & the words tumble forth, hot and urgent as if poured like molten metal into a mold. He insists that Colonel Ladendorf is in fact not himself but rather a walking corpse—a shell— invested by something unclean and incorporeal. The terms he uses are demon, or djinn, in a manner suggesting that to him the words are interchangeable. The thing inside the Dutchman needs flesh to provide its agency in the world. It is spiteful, demented, bent on confusion & chaos. Rivera says Ladendorf turns us against the Arabs and the Arabs against us in turn. He and his kind are acolytes of a theology of Despair. It cannot be written, because the words make no sense. These dark spirits occupy the region & have turned it from Eden to a waste: a land of shattered bones and broken shields. Ghosts wander like wind through the sand, and the dead dream bitter pictures beneath it.

How the Colonel became invested with this foul thing is beyond the priest's ken. He suspects it happened many years past, & that the thing—the "hidden one," or demon—may have spent time in seclusion, dormant, to keep its physical Form from Decay. The demon burns what it touches, including, eventually, its Host. It can be confined by metal, specifically Iron, & in fact it needs this substance in the corpus of its host in order to maintain its Lodgment. It obtains this ferrous element from human blood. This helps to explain the foul murders on our journey, & the disfigurements attending them. The creature needs our fluids. It laps them from the organs it removes from the bodies of its victims, leaving the tissues desiccated and considerably altered in size and color, like the shell of a grape, the contents of which have been evacuated. The importance of the element may also explain the Colonel's odor, much discussed, of knife blades. He smells of the iron he ingests.

The Spaniard thinks the demon has some particular purpose for leading us west, though he cannot say what it is, or if it shall remain the thing's purpose for any length of time in the future. And if reaching Tripoli is its purpose, it must bode ill for us to accomplish it. I note that the priest imparts this information (or speculation) to me grudgingly, as if he is not sure I deserve to know it. He says that MacLeish and I have already thwarted him once, when we rescued the Colonel from a band of vigilantes in Alexandria. The priest had seen evidence of the demon's work in the Christian district of the city, where the creature killed and partially consumed several young girls and left their remains on the steps of the city's oldest church. Rivera assembled a sort of posse to locate the killer, and armed them with iron-tipped staves, laved with holy water. A group of men found, and chased, and proceeded to beat the Colonel with these weapons, but their work was interrupted. By the time the priest and the main body of his deputies arrived on the scene, the Dutchman had been saved from his beating by two men in blue uniforms. Us, the priest says, with evident malice—meaning MacLeish and I. For some time he believed we were in league with the demon, and indeed sought us out in order to try us on this score. But no more. He therefore asks me to aid him in a task the very name of which is enough to accomplish my Death: he asks me to join him in assassinating the Colonel.

Worse—he whispers that I endanger my immortal soul if I do not.

20

Derna

On a bright hot afternoon the expedition makes camp on a bluff overlooking Derna. It is a disappointing sight. The marines have crossed hundreds of miles of desert dragging dreams of plunder behind them. They have mused together on the riches of the Barbary pirates, taken over centuries of theft: diamonds and emeralds, ivory and pearls, Mexican gold and Peruvian silver. But the city is smaller than expected, and much less grand. The would-be conquerors see crooked lanes lined with flat-roofed mud houses. Near the shore a handful of stone warehouses stand white against the brown of the earth and the blue of the sea, and the tips of olive and poplar trees reach above the roofs like tiny flowers. There are two minarets near the northern outskirts of the city. Not far from them rises the city's largest structure, surmised by Luco Androutsos to be the governor's palace.

Lt. Daniel Corrigan

"Might as well sack Brooklyn," says Clay. He was always skinny. The march through the desert has left him almost skeletal.

"And deflower the dusky maidens of Hackensack," adds Stennett. "Goddammit."

Corrigan, Ladendorf, and Sweet are assigned to reconnoiter to the south. Corrigan makes observations from a promontory half a mile shy of the city's outskirts. He takes notes and makes sketches as Ladendorf keeps up a steady stream of commentary. As if to mock Sweet's stiffness in his presence, the Dutchman is elaborately polite. The inhabitants of Cyrenaica, he says, are descended from many races. Among them are Moors or Morelcos, who were driven out of Spain at the end of the fifteenth century, and Arabians who trace their descent from those Mahometans who formerly subdued this region. Levantines, Turks, Jews, and Berbers make up the rest of the population. Arabs and Moors are most numerous, with the latter composing the great body of the inhabitants of the towns.

In the foothills they find an army of sheep. None offers resistance. Ladendorf and Corrigan confer with an elderly Berber who sits on the ruins of an overturned dung cart, scratching the back of his neck with a set of long, twisted fingernails. He says he has been waiting for them, though no one seems to know who he is. He wears a ragged gray robe clotted with mud at the hem. His eyes are crusted with pus, and flies explore them as he speaks.

The man explains that he has been placed here by the governor of Derna to warn the foreign devils. There is no hope of taking the city, he says. The Christians will die in their boots. Their bones will bleach in the sun of Cyrenaica, and their children will forget the names of their fathers.

Corrigan waits patiently to deliver a retort. He says the blessings of democratic civil society are available to those who welcome Prince Ahmad and his army of liberators. There are choices to be made. Progress or privation. Freedom or tyranny. Ladendorf appears to translate. He speaks softly, with little intonation. The Berber seems puzzled. Then stunned. Still Ladendorf speaks. He moves closer, and now closer still, until he is whispering in the old man's ear. The man glances from the Dutchman to the two marines, hatred and disbelief struggling for control of his features. When Ladendorf finishes, the Berber puts his hands to his head. Tears roll down his cheeks.

The Dutchman chuckles.

"What did you tell him?" asks the lieutenant.

"It is of no consequence."

"What did you say, Colonel? I'm afraid I must insist."

"You have no room to *insist* on anything with me, Lieutenant. But calm yourself. I told him that last night I visited his home, which happens to be a stinking shack with a broken door near the governor's stables. I entered the bed of his children. There I found his youngest daughter, his particular favorite, and I spoke with her awhile. She is a pretty thing, a creature of wild dark hair and knobby knees. Leyla, they call her. A voice like a nightingale. As I said, we spoke for a time. Then I reached up between her legs and I dragged her soul out of her body. I have it with me, in a little green bottle I keep in my tent. I like to listen to her sing. And then I told our friend that I could return this soul, or not, depending on his conduct. I also informed him that if I sent for his daughter, she would come to me, and I would do things to her that he would not care to imagine being done to a dog. And then I would cut her throat and send him her eyes as proof that the little nightingale was no more. As you said, Lieutenant. He has a choice. You may ask him anything you wish. He will tell you. I'm sure of it."

"Very droll," says Corrigan. He has gone pale in the heat. "That's not the sort of choice I meant."

"Perhaps not. But it's the only one he understands. He's a peasant. He doesn't care about your theories of governance."

"He can't care if you don't tell him what they are."

"I know these people. I know what they understand. Try him. He'll talk."

Corrigan glances at Sweet. Sweet looks away. He feels vaguely ashamed.

"You have a vivid imagination, sir."

Ladendorf shrugs. "I suspect I do."

"Very well," says the lieutenant. A drop of sweat hanging on his ear catches the sun like a jewel. He addresses the old man as the Dutchman translates. "How are the eastern walls defended?"

The Berber tells all he knows.

* * *

Later that day, Corrigan delivers his report to a council of officers: Weston, Lakos Androutsos, Selim Comb. Governor

Ali Rasmin's defenses include a battery of four twelve-pound field guns situated on the roof of a salt warehouse in the maze of mud buildings in the northeast corner of the city. Along the eastern periphery of town the governor's men have thrown up temporary breastworks: wagons and doors, earthen berms, cloth bags of sand. According to the old Berber, a number of the city's inhabitants loyal to King Yusuf have provided the terraces and walls of their houses with loopholes to allow for musket fire. Finally, the governor has positioned a ten-inch howitzer on the roof of his palace. Ali Rasmin can mobilize perhaps six hundred men in defense of the city. A few will die for him. Most would prefer not to. A fair number couldn't care less which brother rules Tripoli, Ahmad or Yusuf, as long as they are left alone.

Weston is delighted by the reports. In fact, he suggests that no ground fighting need occur. All he requires is the Navy. It is a matter of technology. The inevitability of the governor's downfall may be seen through application of a simple calculus: the destructive power of eighteen-pound shot, multiplied by rates of fire, delivered with an accuracy unmatched by any naval force in the world save perhaps that of Great Britain. *Fury* and *Endeavor* will deliver such a storm of iron and fire that resistance will quickly crumble. While the Arabs are a fierce race, unafraid of bloodshed, they are famously shy of artillery. No Christian lives need be lost. Corrigan nods dutifully. Only Colonel Ladendorf seems disappointed.

* * *

That evening a delegation of sheikhs rides out from town to pay their respects to Ahmad Vartoonian. Carpets are set out on the ground in a circle, so that all assembled may speak as equals. Tea is served, along with pickles and cheeses from *Fury*. Weston sits with his guests and eats with his right hand only, as is the custom in this region.

The talk is cautious and polite. Nothing happens quickly in the desert. The sheikhs remember signs of favor Prince Ahmad's father showed the province when he ruled Tripoli. Yusuf's seizure of power is lamentable. Their loyalty to Ahmad, the eldest son and rightful ruler, is not to be doubted. But the facts speak for themselves. More reinforcements arrived yesterday from Benghazi, and some say the governor can now bring eight hundred men, regulars and militia, into battle. Ali Rasmin is a grasping, profane individual. None here bear him any love. However, as he possesses cannons, the breastworks, and a much larger force of soldiers, the sheikhs opine that the Americans will find it difficult to dislodge him. Many will die. It all seems so... *unnecessary.*

Weston grows impatient with the proceedings. He has guessed the intentions of these visitors, and the origins of their mission. He therefore reprises his earlier speech. Numbers. Physics. The iron laws of mass and force. This audience is less impressed with the lecture. From his position in back of the general, Sweet watches the proceedings carefully. He observes Prince Ahmad in particular. It is clear the rightful ruler of Tripoli wishes he was back in Egypt, eating wild plums.

* * *

The next day passes slowly. There is no sign of the Navy, but Derna is bustling. The city's eastern defenses are inspected by the governor's men and portions of them strengthened. General Weston orders that a fire be maintained on the highest point of the bluffs overlooking the sea. He sends smoke signals into the sky. At two p.m. *Fury* heaves into sight. At four, messages are exchanged by semaphore, and at six, Weston sends a letter back with the boat that has rowed to shore. He includes details from Corrigan's report—layout of the town; suspected battery positions—and his own anticipated line of advance. He implores the Navy to spare the city's Old Mosque, an elaborate structure boasting forty-two cupolas, much revered by the inhabitants. The approximate position of the mosque is marked in red on the lieutenant's sketch of the town. The general proposes to attack tomorrow if *Endeavor* stands in.

Weston next dispatches a letter to the Governor of Cyrenaica. There is no need for bloodshed, he writes. He asks only for a pledge of fealty from Ali Rasmin and safe passage through the province for the rightful ruler of Tripoli, His Royal Highness Prince Ahmad Vartoonian. The expedition will take nothing from the city save what it requires to provision itself for the march west, with fair recompense to be made as soon as practicable. While no man will be pressed into service, Prince Ahmad will gladly accept all volunteers who wish to join him in his advance on Tripoli. Weston warns the governor that any delay in responding to this message will incur the risk of naval bombardment, which may commence as early as the next morning.

The note is returned two hours later. Ali Rasmin's courier gallops back out of camp without waiting for a response. Weston reads the message. He nods. Holding it up, he translates aloud for all who care to hear.

"It's from the Governor," he says. "It reads: YOUR HEAD OR MINE."

Repentance Moore offer his own translation. "Look to your powder, boys. The bastards want a fight."

From the Diary of Lemuel Sweet, May 2, 1805

I have of course dismissed any talk of doing harm to the Colonel. A Court Martial involving evidence that I have even entertained this notion would be enough to lead to my DEATH. If anyone is reading these words, know that I instantly rejected the Spaniard's exhortations on this subject. He therefore turned to discussion of what he believes to be the source of evil & discord in our midst, & an alternative means for addressing it.

He admits that killing Ladendorf would be both difficult, as the spirit inside him is cunning, and possibly fruitless, as the body of the Dutchman is only a temporary vessel for the flame that burns within. He proposes instead a sort of forcible eviction of the demon from its human host. He has with him oddments of the Romish faith: a crucifix, Holy Water, & the like, as well as a copy of the Rituale Romanum, which contains the Ceremony that he says may allow him to force the creature out of Ladendorf's form and banish it to its infernal home.

He does not fear for Ladendorf per se. What we know as the Colonel is long dead, he says, and his soul entirely consumed. The monster must either be driven from the body or buried with it, in a deep hole, surrounded by metal. There was in former days a church in Derna—it has not been heard from in years—where he hopes to enlist the aid of another of his kind. He says Derna was once a Christian city, and home to several of the Brotherhood, a group of men dedicated to the extinction of unholy spirits & other threats to the races of the world. We must therefore get inside the City, if we are to thwart the thing that travels with us. What is to happen next is unclear to me, and the priest seems unwilling to discuss it.

He has asked me on several occasions about the ruby ring the Colonel carries with him. I have answered as best I could, & I admit that I have felt relief at being able to discuss with some candor my dealings with the Dutchman.

Rivera asks why I did not take the ring when it was offered to me. I find it difficult to answer, tho in truth I believe it would have been folly to enter into the debt of so dubious a creature as the Colonel, as I suspect he wants an item in return that I must not give. The priest urges me not to repeat my mistake. If the ring is within my grasp again, he says, take it, and bring it to him. Is Rome not rich enough already? I ask. His answer is fierce. It is not a matter of wealth, he claims. It is a matter of safety—for all of us. The ring was created for an ancient king and delivered to him by agents of the Almighty. It holds powers I cannot understand. The Church has been searching for it for centuries. While Ladendorf sees the thing as a bauble and a means of seduction, he is bound to pass it on to more dangerous members of his Hellish Tribe, who will use the ring to calamitous effect. But when pressed, the priest will explain no further.

I am frustrated in my attempts to test my understanding of these matters. MacLeish has since his flogging seemingly sworn enmity with all his former friends, though his disgust focuses in particular on the General. In this I try to tell him he is misguided: the General had little choice but to order punishment in the matter of the poniard, and the sentence could indeed have been the ultimate sanction. MacLeish will hear none of it. He waves me away, and has threatened to clout me again. Though his back has scabbed, thanks to the doctor's good ministry, his resentment festers. I have no way to speak with him about either the Colonel or the priest. Likewise, Prejean is too timid a soul for such conversation, and Stennett a notorious wag-tongue, unable to keep a confidence. These are my closest companions on the expedition, and none fits my need. The sense of the peril I face is matched only by my isolation. Are Rivera and Ladendorf really delegates of the forces of good and evil, as the priest himself suggests? Or are they both lunatics? And, given what I think I've seen and heard, have I taken leave of my senses as well? I would not entertain the priest's suspicions for a moment, were it not for my experience of abandonment—and rescue— in the desert. While it seems unreal to me now, a sort of delusional interlude, the burns and scratches linger on my skin, and my nightmares continue unabated. I fear I am close to my breaking point.

21.

Combat

In cold metal darkness before dawn Lieutenant Corrigan assembles his Immortals: the eight marines, the Greeks, half the Egyptians, and a score of Bedouin foot soldiers, these last armed only with swords and spears. All told, they are seventy men. Four mules pull the field piece, a twelve-pounder rowed ashore the previous afternoon from *Fury*. The company marches across the highlands and down through wrinkled hills and a field of barley to take up position in a shallow wash only a hundred yards from Derna's makeshift ramparts. They deploy in a long thin line, six paces between each man. Corrigan crosses himself. It is the first time any of them have seen a sign of reverence from the lieutenant. The Egyptians murmur in prayer. Sweet conjures up an image of his mother and tries to hold it, as if by preserving this picture he could hold time still—and perhaps preserve himself. It doesn't work. He cannot keep her face in view. It does not seem like a good omen.

The sun comes up and the city reveals itself. A flock of birds moves north, a shimmering tapestry of blue and brown.

MacLeish returns to the line, buttoning his britches.

"Goddamned squids. The hell are they waitin' for?" He nods at the bay. Half a mile distant, the two American ships sit like tiny models on the sea.

As if on cue, *Endeavor* spits fire. Moments later the sound of the frigate's broadside thunders across the water like the bark of some predatory animal grown impossibly in scale and menace. The iron balls smash into the stone and mud walls of the city and after this first outburst there is an interval of silence, as if all involved are attempting to calibrate the balance of forces arrayed in the field. Then, from Derna, comes a cry of defiance. It is taken up from a number of positions. It grows louder. Now

Fury. The two ships fire together. There is no hurry. Roar after roar: a dozen broadsides. The air is calm. *Endeavor* periodically disappears in a cloud of her own powder smoke.

For three hours the pounding continues. Damnation in the air. The footsteps of titans. At mid-morning the marines eat hardtack and a ration of beef. An Arab boy brings a pail of water down the line, hunching his shoulders every time he hears a blast. The heat has grown fierce by the time General Weston arrives to confer with Corrigan. Sweet wipes his face on his sleeve. And here too is Ladendorf, clad as usual in his white linen blouse and as cheerful as ever. He stops to converse with the men, each in his own tongue. *It will be a bloodbath,* he murmurs. *The townspeople have sworn they will show us no mercy. I've seen what they do to good Christians. Hack men, women, and children to pieces, and feed the bodies to the dogs...*

A moment later, the lieutenant orders a volley. The marines' twelve-pounder fires high. A spattering of musket fire responds from the *barricado,* and there are shouts from behind the mud walls. Sweet sees heads moving above the ramparts, but he is still loading. He fires. Tears open a cartridge with his teeth. *Powder in the pan. Cartridge in the barrel. Ball. Wadding. Ram. Cock the hammer.* He fires again. He can hear the bones of the city being shattered by the giant iron projectiles of the Navy. Distant cries of anger and anguish drift on the wind. Somewhere a bell is ringing. Repentance Moore is taking his time. The Virginian loads the Dickert rifle deliberately, carefully measuring his powder. He kills two men with shots to the head. The defenders of Derna learn not to peer over their breastworks. But the musket fire from the mud walls grows insistent nevertheless. Just a few feet away from Sweet, an Egyptian is pierced through the throat. He tries to tell his companion, but the companion turns away. There is no screaming, only a tremendous gout of blood. A hole in the windpipe means a quiet death.

A musket ball takes Stephen Prejean's high-crowned hat. Another kicks up the dirt in front of him. Two of the Greeks look down the line, their heads inclined against the firing as if it were a sudden rain. Another man falls, this one outwardly unmarked, as if the mechanics of his end were bypassed by a fate unconcerned with method or motive but intent only on a final tallying of accounts. Sweet hears the blast of the field piece. Two halves of a wooden pole spin lazily up into the air and fall to earth fifty yards away. There are curses around him. The gunner, a Greek, forgot to remove the rammer before firing. It is lost to them now, and the cannon as well, since the charge can no longer be properly set.

The sun crawls under their collars. Sweet's head is wet with sweat, and the steel barrel of his musket boils the moisture where it drips. Another ball zips past his ear. Though the American ships continue to pour fire on the town, it is unmistakable. The defense along Derna's eastern wall has grown stronger.

"No ground fighting necessary," says MacLeish in falsetto. "A simple matter of goddamn *mathematics.*"

Sweet nods, but it's no use. MacLeish ignores the gesture.

At noon, a pause. The men look up, confused. Behind them, the prince's cavalry advances toward the southeastern corner of the city. Led by Sheikh al-Tahib and Selim Comb, the riders hold green and black flags with the words of the Prophet flickering like fiery runes upon them. The horses race each other in front of a cloud of fine dust. The marines turn to watch. It is a magnificent sight. General Weston cheers as he waves his hat.

"Bayonets," says Corrigan.

Sweet's stomach clenches.

"Christ Almighty," says MacLeish. "Didn't think he had it in him."

The orders go down the line, echoed in Copt and Greek and Arabic.

Corrigan again. "Charge your muskets. Prepare to advance. Mr. O'Dell?"

"Sir."

"Ready the air rifle, if you please. Not to be fired until we're within the walls. Do you understand?"

"Aye, sir."

"And then to be fired with extreme rapidity. Let them know we've arrived."

"Aye, sir."

The lieutenant gazes at the defenses in front of them. He draws his sword.

"God and your mothers are watching, gentlemen. Do your duty. Remember the *Charleston*. Kill them all."

It is a moment worth pondering. Life and death, so perfectly balanced. Sweet has no way of knowing which is stronger. But there is no time for reflection. There is never time, he realizes. General Weston is ten yards out in front already, scimitar in one hand, pistol in the other, striding toward the enemy like a farmer out to kill a fox.

"Crazy bastard," says Stennett.

Corrigan screams something, then follows. And Lemuel Sweet is running.

* * *

He crosses the long yards of dirt and goat dung in under a minute with powder smoke burning his eyes and marines on either side of him gasping for air. He can hear the cries of the Greeks. *Blood and fire*, he thinks. *Released at last. They're enjoying this.* He mounts the low stone rampart, halts, leaps away from the arc of a blade. Sweet's attacker lunges forward, but the stones of the wall shift and slide to the ground. The Arab—a sharp-nosed little man in dirty robes and a blue turban—lands awkwardly. His left leg is broken.

Before he can think of what he should do, Sweet shoves his bayonet into the little man's belly. He is surprised by how easily it slides in. Still, it is not the ideal spot. Hollis Mason has warned his companions that a man stabbed in the gut will seize the musket barrel, holding his assailant in place. Sure enough, it happens here. The Arab shrieks as Sweet struggles to free the triangular blade. A boy leaps onto the marine's back and claws at his eyes. Sweet shrugs him off. One of the Greeks is screaming at him, but he can't understand the words. The Greek dispatches Sweet's attacker with a pistol butt to the side of the head. The kid stumbles away, and the Greek pursues. When the boy falls, the Greek slits his throat, and then hurries over to dispatch the wounded Arab in similar fashion. Sweet takes his weapon back, turns to advance. The Greek pantomimes the act of firing the musket to free it from the grip of an enemy, and the private finally comprehends.

The defenders of Derna flee in front of him. *Around the corner. Up an alley.* The air is brown and red and some flashing metallic white that may be the color of sun. He sees dust and smoke and hears musket balls sizzling through the air like angry bees. *Forward.* This is all he knows. Fear and adrenaline have squeezed every other thought out of his mind. He has a blinding headache. He wants to run. He needs to rest. He wants to scream. But it doesn't matter what he wants. Sweet takes another man with the bayonet. It is a protracted struggle, demeaning and odd. Curses ride the bubbles of blood that seep from the man's mouth. Sweet is slick with sweat. He fires the musket and sure enough, he is able to remove it from the hole in his enemy's belly. He knows he should finish the man—club him to death; shoot him in the face—but something won't let him. Perhaps God will do it instead. Leave a letter of apology. Forgive both men their sins. Sweet walks another three steps and has to stop to empty his stomach.

MacLeish appears. His face is black with gunpowder and grime, the whites of his eyes and teeth unnaturally bright by comparison. He emerges from the smoke of battle like some pitch-darkened denizen of hell loping untrammeled by obedience to any watchful god or moral precept and set loose on earth like malice made animate. Sweet's best friend on earth. *Grinning. Exultant.* He holds a severed head.

"I heard the old man wants *proof.*"

"Of what?"

MacLeish shrugs.

"How much further?" asks Sweet.

"The battery. Two streets up."

MacLeish sets his grisly trophy beneath a donkey cart and settles a palm frond over it. The dark face stares wide-eyed in death, as if disbelieving a world that could see it leave and not even shrug.

MacLeish warns an Egyptian: "Don't take my head."

The marines see Corrigan, Prejean, and three Greeks moving ahead of them. They hurry to catch up. A mule lies dead in an alley, a bouquet of flowers in its mouth, its intestines strewn beside the body. A pack of monkeys goes galloping down the dirt street, wide-eyed with alarm. A little girl looks out from behind a door.

"Get *back*," hisses Sweet. He makes a pushing motion with his right arm, but the girl doesn't move. Lieutenant Corrigan waves them forward. The front of his blue jacket is so drenched in red that Sweet thinks the man is dying. A misperception. Corrigan pulls him close. His voice, generally mellifluous, has been coarsely shredded.

"All of us. Around the corner and up the steps. Take the guns."

Stennett and O'Dell join them, along with two of the Egyptians. Now they are nine. They pause to charge and prime their weapons. Then they move low around the corner and sprint up the street. An Arab at the top of the steps sees them coming. He levels his musket. They see a flash, and O'Dell goes down.

MacLeish bellows like a branded bull. The Arab runs. A dozen of his comrades man the cannons, but only two are still firing. Bodies and broken stone litter the roof, and a severed arm hangs out of a wooden bushel. The cannoneers' muskets lie nearby, and the defenders of Derna move to retrieve them, but it is too late. Corrigan kills with the sword, MacLeish with the bayonet. The Greeks use pistols and knives.

A projectile smashes into the building beside them, destroying the wall.

"Sons of whores," shouts Corrigan. "Our own ships! Raise the flag."

"Raise it from what?" says Sweet.

"Jesus. *Wave it,* goddammit! Before they blow us to pieces." Corrigan pulls the standard from his jacket. It is stained with blood. Sweet unfurls the Stars and Stripes and shakes it above his head. Another puff of smoke floats away from the *Fury,* but the ball passes high. The cannonade ceases.

The marines turn the serviceable guns west. The Governor's palace stands in this direction, but it is no use: the warehouse roof is too low, and they are unable to spot the target. Corrigan leaves Stennett in charge of the battery, with instructions to spike the guns if they are in danger of being retaken. Sweet follows the lieutenant and MacLeish into the streets, but there is no enemy to be found, only frightened animals and demolished mud houses.

At three o'clock they meet up with an Egyptian infantryman who has been sent by the general to summon his army to the center of the city. Selim Comb and Sheikh al-Tahib have routed the Tripolitan cavalry, the Egyptian reports. Prince Ahmad rode with his men, but had to be lashed to the saddle. It is said that he stayed as far to the rear of the column as he could. It is one of the few blots on the day. Snipers still fire from doorways and windows, but by evening the bulk of the forces loyal to King Yusuf and the Governor have either fled the city or reconsidered their allegiances. The Greeks go door to door. They have lost eight of their comrades. They pull their enemies into the streets and club or stab them to death. By midnight there are seventy heads on display in front of the Governor's palace. Several are female. Some have been scalped. Derna has fallen. The governor is said to be hiding, and no one wonders why. America has taken a piece of Africa.

* * *

There is another fatality of the siege to report. This one is the subject of revulsion and rumor. The naked body of Senor Alfonse Campos Rivera is found late in the afternoon. His throat has been slashed, a customary Arab method of homicide, and his eyes have been clawed from their sockets. More curious: the Spaniard's pale corpse is lashed upside-down to a wooden post that has been planted in a goat pen near the southern market. Lieutenant Corrigan speculates that Senor Rivera must have been killed elsewhere. For one thing, no one in the neighborhood will admit to having witnessed the crime. For another, despite the ragged hole in Rivera's throat, there is no blood to be seen on the ground nearby—though the Spaniard's head is so covered in gore that the man's features are hard to make out. Painted in mud or dung on the corpse are tiny angular letters of some obscure language, interspersed with fanciful whorls and stars. A silver crucifix has been jammed into the dead man's rectum up to the cross bar. In his mouth are found several crumpled sheets of paper—pages Corrigan identifies as coming from the *Rituale Romanum*.

"Savages," growls MacLeish, observing the body. "We should kill the lot."

The big man glances at Colonel Ladendorf. Sweet sees the exchange, and feels his heart skip a beat. He could swear the two men share a wink.

22.

The Sheikh of Misreat

The next day General Weston and Prince Ahmad tour the conquered city as its liberated citizens exalt them. Women ululate on the rooftops. The names of the conquerors are shouted in the streets, and the prince's personal flag is raised above the cratered palace. Local merchants bring tributes of dates and silks, baskets of figs and olives and oranges.

Ahmad is delighted. He smiles and waves to the townspeople, and speaks of establishing his government in Derna. It has a protected harbor, after all, and cultivated fields to the west. The forested highlands would make a splendid site for a summer residence. Weston listens to such talk with difficulty. He reminds His Eminence that the war has only just begun. Three hundred American sailors are still in prison six hundred miles to the west, subject to the whims of a madman and his sorceress. The first order of duty is to raise a battalion of fresh recruits from among the citizens of Derna and the outlying provinces. They will need to at least double the size of their force to capture Benghazi.

"Of course," says Ahmad. "Benghazi."

* * *

Weston learns that Governor Ali Rasmin has been granted asylum in the home of the Sheikh of Misreat, an ancient chief who is much venerated in the city. This seems at first blush to be a stroke of good fortune: a prisoner of rank, with which to negotiate with King Yusuf. But neither promises nor threats can persuade the sheikh to expel the governor from the premises. The old man is frail but resolute. He is nearly blind, and is escorted to the front gate of his home by one of his grandsons. Though he has no particular love for the governor, the sheikh declares that he will not allow the hospitality of his house to be violated. He urges that whatever may be the weakness or even the crimes of the Arabs, there was never an instance known among them of giving up a fugitive to whom they have once accorded their protection. If he were to violate this sacred principle, the vengeance of Allah and the odium of all mankind might justly fix upon him and his posterity.

"And the guns of two American warships shall fix upon you if you do not," says Weston.

The sheikh shrugs. It seems clear which peril he would rather face.

✿ ✿ ✿

The next morning an army gathers at the base of the highlands east of the city, arrayed for battle. There is much confusion. In only a day, the forces of the warring Vartoonian brothers have reversed position. Attacker is now defender, and vice versa. Weston deploys his infantrymen on the eastern ramparts. The marines hold the center, sharing the breastworks with citizens of Derna whom they strongly suspect were trying to kill them earlier in the week.

The natives are liberal in their loyalties. Most are poor shots, mostly because they load their muskets with nails and stones. Still, they bustle about, and brandish their antique scimitars in defiant and threatening attitudes. Weston fires the howitzer from its newly fortified location. At noon, a charge: the enemy stir up dust, but cannot bring themselves to meet the vast number of townspeople who have apparently declared themselves for Prince Ahmad. The advance falters three hundred yards from the city walls. There, while their officers confer, the foot soldiers ease themselves to the ground and wait. An hour later, the army retires. Some of the townspeople jeer at the retreat. The marines simply watch.

* * *

General Weston spends the next three days putting Derna in a proper state of defense. Trenches are dug and picket lines established, and additional firing ports are drilled in the sturdier mud structures on the northern and eastern edges of town. The Greeks and Egyptians bury their fallen. Weston performs services for Privates Morris O'Dell and Moses Clay. O'Dell died quickly, with a musket ball through one eye. The automatic air rifle was evidently taken from him where he lay. Since the looters discarded the spare air reservoirs, however, the weapon is now of no use save as a curiosity.

Private Clay's death was prolonged. He ventured off one of Derna's three principal thoroughfares into a blind alley, where he and a Greek sergeant were trapped in a tanner's yard by a group of King Yusuf's supporters and hacked to pieces. Both bodies are badly burned. One of Clay's legs is still missing. Indeed, there is little of the man left to bury.

* * *

During the week, the governor's forces are reinforced twice. Some of the townspeople are said to be confused. No one knows which is the stronger party. The governor's army is larger, but Prince Ahmad has Derna, the howitzer, and two American warships anchored just offshore. And there is a rumor circulating in the city. On the day of the attack, a number of the eastern wall's defenders claim to have seen riders advancing behind the marines: a dozen or more cavalrymen, clad in iron armor like western knights of old and impervious to musket fire. The sight was so uncanny that it caused some of the city's garrison to flee.

Weston chuckles at the tale. "A cavalry of phantoms," he muses. "We'd have paid well for such assistance. I don't recall that any was offered."

The enemy have since their eviction from Derna been endeavoring to corrupt and bring over the townspeople to their side. They send women and children into the city with promises of gold for those who will desert and warnings of death for those who will not. Anyone found wearing the

Americans' tri-cornered hats will be executed on the spot. This is a pointless threat. While the marines have managed to give away fifty-three hats, they have yet to see anyone wearing one.

Governor Ali Rasmin is now classified by General Weston as an active enemy, entitled to none of the privileges of Arab hospitality. As the Sheikh of Misreat remains immovable in his resolution not to give the man up for trial, Weston tries an experiment. He marches into the neighborhood at the head of thirty-two Christians, bayonets fixed, and declares his intention to take Ali Rasmin from his sanctuary by force. A general alarm spreads through the quarter. It is said the foreigners no longer respect the customs of Tripoli and the laws of the desert. Weston urges in response that as the Governor is an outlaw, he has forfeited his right to protection. He has been beaten from his post but is still resident in a conquered town, and is therefore Weston's prisoner by all the laws of war. If Ali Rasmin claims refuge under the banners of his faith, he should live peaceably, according to its teachings. In truth, however, the man is carrying on war against Prince Ahmad even in his place of hiding. By doing so, he has forfeited the leniency due to a prisoner. Weston will therefore have him dead or alive.

It is said that Weston might have read law, had he not chosen military pursuits. The elderly sheikh expresses admiration for the general's powers of masculine expression, but remains inflexible. He will not give up the governor. Outside there is shouting. Corrigan reports that the neighborhood is mobilizing to defend its head man's convictions. Prince Ahmad implores Weston to put off his attempt until tomorrow, promising to use his best efforts in the meantime to draw Ali Rasmin from the protection of the sheikh by gentler means.

Weston relents. He withdraws his troops, well satisfied with his display of might. That evening, the Sheikh of Misreat assists the Governor in escaping to the enemy camp, with a number of fighting men at his side.

From the Diary of Lemuel Sweet, May 5, 1805

I write tonight in hopes that reducing my torments to paper will diminish their power. I had expected that combat would cure me of my fears and uncertainties. To the contrary, it has simply substituted one set of miseries for another. Where once I doubted I could kill another man, and rebuked myself as a coward, now I know that I can—and it is a mystery to me which state is worse. In sleep I have seen the same scene on several occasions. I spy a young girl, dark-haired and brown-eyed, pretty like my Clara. She stands alone in an alley, and when she sees me she holds out a red flower. I am to take it. This much is clear. But when I reach out to grasp the bud, the girl disappears, and in my hand I hold a serpent instead. I try to fling the creature from me, but it wraps itself around my arms, and will not be disposed of. Now it binds my wrists together, and spirals up toward my face. The snake rears back to strike, and then I wake up. Always sweating. Once I voided the contents of my stomach with such violence that Dr. Rizzolo was summoned. I have asked him for a draught to deliver me from this vision, but so far he has been unable or unwilling to provide such a concoction. And so I sleep but little, and not well.

Other troubles. Tucked into my bedroll I have found a note from my late acquaintance and tormentor, Padre Rivera. It is an extraordinary document, dated from the morning of our assault on the city. In broken English he writes to tell me he fears for his life. The Dutchman has been to visit him—in consequence of which, he says, he feels he must make all clear to me while he can. First, the ring—

The inhabitants of the so-called lost city of Zerzura were not lost at all, he writes. They were vassals of a man named Geoffrey of Bulmershe, a grim and implacable follower of the faith who did terrible things in the name of the Cross. They paid dearly for their cruelty and avarice. When the knights of the First Crusade took Jerusalem, they killed Mahometans and Jews alike, men and women and children. They killed until they waded in blood. Some helped themselves to the treasures of the city. And others went further: down deep below the sacred temple, where many mystical relics and heirlooms had been kept secret for centuries. Sir Geoffrey took the holiest item of all: an iron ring given to King Solomon by the archangel Michael, inscribed with Hebrew lettering, & bearing a six-pointed talisman of such power and authority that the king could command even the spirits of the earth and air to do his bidding. It was this ring that Geoffrey took from Jerusalem. For this sacrilege the knight and all who traveled with him were cursed. God sent them into the desert and there pronounced their doom. As Geoffrey had presumed to possess the Seal of Solomon, he was granted his wish. He and his crusaders were charged with protecting the ring for a thousand years. If they failed, their souls would wander in hell forever.

They protected it well, these men. They clad it in gold and hid the lettering with a ruby, which proclaimed the item's value but obscured its significance. Alas, the ring was taken by a thief many centuries ago—a man rescued by the knights from certain death in the desert. It passed into the hands of the Emir of Benghazi, and was stolen from him in turn. The thing we know as Colonel Ladendorf travels with this ring and uses its great beauty to seduce his victims. And yet not even this infernal creature knows the ring's real powers, which can only be wielded by one who can speak the letters hidden beneath the gem, which spell out the name of God. Perhaps it was the demon who stole the ring from the Emir of Benghazi so many years ago. And perhaps it was the demon also, in one or another of his human forms, who falsely told the emir that he could find the ring in Zerzura, where a band of heretics and thieves hid in the desert with his stolen treasure. The emir rode out with his army the next day. He took Zerzura by surprise, and slaughtered all within, no matter their age or gender. The little village was searched inside and out, but in vain, for no ring was found. The emir returned to Benghazi with nothing to show for his efforts but the Christian blood on his sword.

The bones of the Crusaders who lived in Zerzura have long since turned to dust. But Padre Rivera says their spirits roam the empty lands to retrieve what was taken from them.

They despise thieves, and execute them whenever they find them. And yet they have but one true mission: to recover the ring, and hide the Seal of Solomon where it will never again be found. It was this ring that the priest was after, in order to bring it to the safety &custody of the Roman Church. And yet he leaves me no instructions, only a blessing, and a request that I pray to invoke the assistance of powers greater than my own. I am therefore no further along my path than before. Further back, perhaps—as I know what to do, but not how to do it. The situation confounds me. Aside from the practical difficulties I face, I find myself confused on some deeper level as well. Is it possible I have misjudged the extent of man's capacity to understand the workings of the world? Are there indeed things strange and unholy that exist outside our ability to comprehend them? And what harm could it do to follow the Spaniard's imprecation, and ask the aid of a higher intelligence—and deeper mercy?

Unfortunately, I do not know what prayers would avail me in my current situation. I have not spent any great amount of my time in such pursuits, which I always deemed fanciful and unproductive. If I only knew the proper steps, I am afraid I would be tempted to cast aside my faith in Reason and, however reluctantly, seek solace in the Irrational. But knowing them not, I continue on with my trust in the revelations of Science intact, confident they will bring me to a satisfactory understanding of my route to safety, and the manner in which I can best protect my comrades—and myself—from harm. I will therefore resist the inclination to follow the priest's final directive to me, scrawled in a hasty post-script.

FOR THE LOVE OF GOD, he writes. FLEE.

23.

The Poison Wind

Now the desert takes them in. A storm from the south brings a shoulder of sand half a mile high and as far across as the eye can see, advancing out of the wasteland like a yellow wall of surf. Locals call this phenomenon the *simum*—the poison wind. The fine dust sets the Christians' teeth on edge. There is sand in everything, grit in all they eat. Palm trees rustle and shake in the tempest and the world is without form, as if all echoes of the Almighty's ordering strictures uttered at and in creation of Creation itself have finally trailed off into corridors of nothingness beyond light and human hope and the motes and atoms and elemental stuff of existence, unbound at last, have devolved immediately into mere random movement now and for the rest of eternity hot and howling and corrosive to the touch. The Americans wrap cloth around their faces for fear of losing their sight to the wind-driven particles, and they move through the streets laterally, with one hand raised as if to ward off this prolonged and awful judgment of the sky.

Sweet does not see MacLeish for two days. Prejean says he keeps company with the Dutchman, who has General Weston's permission to use the private as a personal bodyguard. While the big man seems content to accompany Colonel Ladendorf, he is increasingly disdainful of Corrigan and his fellow marines. This is unfortunate, as the marines need all the help they can get. Assassins haunt the empty streets, lethal and anonymous in the haze. There is no way to tell friend from foe. The second night of the storm, two of the Egyptians are found with their throats cut, the bloody genitals of dogs stuffed in their mouths. The Egyptians were on sentinel duty only a few yards from the marine bivouac.

Weston orders a curfew and doubles the guard. One of the Governor's spies is found near the magazine. He is a twelve year-old Arab boy with only three teeth. Still smarting from his humiliation at the hands of the Sheikh of Misreat, Weston orders summary execution. Private MacLeish hears of the sentence, and volunteers to carry it out. Due to the swirling dust, he must fire on the boy at a distance of only ten feet. The boy prays loudly in Arabic. When someone calls to him, he turns and runs. MacLeish's musket ball severs his spine, and the little Arab lies in the street, unable to move, until the private puts another ball through the back of his skull. He is so close when he discharges his weapon that the boy's hair catches fire, and the head smolders until wind-blown sand puts it out. By dusk the corpse is covered in an inch of desert, and no one has come forward to claim it.

Murder is suddenly commonplace. Residents of the city say some of the deaths result from long-standing tribal feuds, held in check by Ali Rasmin's constables until the Christians came, now let loose to rage again. The bodies of a prominent spice trader and two of his cousins are found in the city's largest cemetery, covered in goat dung, their hands bound and their throats slashed. A Shiite teenager, one of only a few of these heretics in the city, is beaten to death with clubs and stones. His disfigured corpse is left in the marketplace for all to see, next to a hastily painted wooden sign explaining the boy's sins against God and the Prophet. Some believe Sheikh al-Tahib's men are the killers. The sheikh refuses to discuss the matter with Weston, saying only that the laws of God are no business of the Americans. The general shakes his head. Saddened by the bloodshed, he is nevertheless confident that once the rudiments of democratic self-rule are introduced to the citizens of Derna, much of this secular strife will disappear.

More troubling are the deaths the locals only whisper about. They seem unrelated to any clan dispute or religious schism. Three girls, ages eight to twelve, have been found in wells or hidden in walls, their organs ripped from their bodies, their corpses drained of blood. There are rumors that the Christians are behind it. Indeed, one of their number has been seen in the twilight hours moving silently through the city, amber eyes gazing out from beneath his cloak.

* * *

At dawn the following day, with the dust a brown cloud moving northward over the sea, the enemy appear again in force. They file down from the highlands and form ranks a few hundred yards east of town. Corrigan estimates the governor has a thousand foot soldiers and another four hundred men on horse and camel. It will be a desperate fight. Dr. Rizzolo drafts a codicil to his will. But by ten a.m., inexplicably, the enemy ranks have dissolved.

Weston holds all in readiness. The haze is gone, but the heat persists; the horizon seems to ripple and bend. A defector from the enemy camp states that it was the intention of the governor to have attacked this morning, but the Bedouin under his command refused to fight. The governor demanded that the tribesmen move their camels to the front and flanks, to absorb the enemy's fire. This they declined to do. The governor then issued orders for a general advance. Again the desert dwellers refused, explaining that they had not only the preservation of their own lives but the existence of their families to keep in view. Prince Ahmad has possession of the town, and his Christian allies man several cannons inside the walls of Derna; these, with the great guns of the American warships, would destroy anything that approached.

The Bedouin propose instead to remain in camp until artillery arrives from Tripoli to even the odds. Then, they promise, they will happily kill the pretender to King Yusuf's throne and slaughter his lackeys, who are said to have brought evil spirits to the region to torment the faithful. And of course there remains the prospect that the Christians will leave the city and attempt to renew their march west toward Tripoli. Once outside the walls of Derna, they will be easy prey. Thus, an uneasy stalemate has set in. While the governor has been obliged to give up the prospect of a rapid victory, he seems content to wait. Day by day, his forces grow stronger.

* * *

The next morning a woman who has been to trade with Ali Rasmin's army states that a detachment of fifty cavalrymen has joined the governor's forces. Ali Rasmin expects four cannons to arrive today or tomorrow, at which point he is confident he will be able to retake the city. His newest troops have promised to cut off the Americans' heads and fire them at the frigates. All who favor Prince Ahmad will be put to death, and their wives and children sold into slavery.

Weston pretends amusement.

"Tell them this," he says, "if you should cross the path of the governor's men again. Tell Mr. Ali Rasmin and his battalion of bootlickers that we Americans have come to this land to spread liberty and the rule of law, and to put a stop once and for all to the violence and unrest in this region. We are establishing a school for the instruction of civics and the physical sciences, and have drawn up instructions that will allow Prince Ahmad's supporters to hold elections for certain municipal posts within the next ninety days. A bill of rights has been drafted for consideration by the people of the province, and approved in principle by both myself and the prince. Tell them that while we Americans welcome peace, we are fierce warriors, who have taken the scalps of many brave enemies, including Mohawks, Shawnees, and Senecas, and that we will not quit the field until our bayonets have tasted Ali Rasmin's blood. Tell the governor that we have conquered the forces of Great Britain, the mightiest power in the world, and that we do not shrink from the challenges of a usurper and patricide who consults with witches, or an army that hides behind camels. Tell them the United States Navy is bombarding Tripoli even as we speak, and preparing to land a force of four hundred marines at the foot of the Red Fortress. Marines, mind you! Men of steel and stone and holy fire. Men who would spit in the eye of Hercules and fight a tempest with a tomahawk. Tell the governor that surrender on my terms is his only hope of survival. Tell him his squalid little circus is coming to an end."

Colonel Ladendorf claps his hands. There is more carnage to come. The Dutchman is delighted.

24.

The Letter

Disaster strikes on May 22nd. A dispatch from Admiral Barron, relayed by *Endeavor*, throws Weston into despair. Weston typically reacts to adversity with anger, imprecations, redoubled effort. This news unmans him—possibly because there is nothing he can do about it.

Operating in Tripoli under a flag of truce, U.S. Ambassador Tobias Lear has concluded a peace treaty with Yusuf Vartoonian. The crew of the *Charleston* is to be freed in return for a ransom of $290 per man, payable in silver, plus delivery of forty tons of Georgia oak for mercantile ship-building purposes: futtocks, hawser pieces, bow timbers and stanchions. King Yusuf has also entered into certain agreements acknowledging the trading rights of U.S. merchant vessels in the Mediterranean, with ancillary covenants establishing codes of salvage and maritime recoupment. Hostilities are to cease immediately. Admiral Barron instructs Mr. Weston— for certainly he is no longer to be addressed as a general officer—to terminate his investment of Derna, and to make arrangements to remove Prince Ahmad and his advisors from the country at the earliest opportunity. The Christians may be taken off as well, of course, but all other members of the expedition are to be left in Derna for reconciliation with their rightful government.

In his confusion the general speaks directly to Sweet, who is standing sentry outside the ruined palace Weston has made his headquarters.

"Reconciliation?" he asks.

Sweet doesn't know how to answer.

The general continues. "I feared this day might come, but I never quite believed it. Our greatest enemy our own government! Can you credit it? Tobias Lear. I hope he and all his backstabbing diplomat friends rot in hell for this. Washington is a rat's nest, Private. With another hundred marines and proper naval support, we could take this whole country, and punish anyone who dares to take up arms against America."

Weston gazes across the square toward where several of Sheikh al-Tahib's men have gathered to eat their evening meal.

"These people who helped us. Who helped the prince. We might as well stick a knife in their backs. This means the death of every one of them."

"Sir," says Sweet.

"Every goddamned *one*," the general snarls, as if the private dared to disagree.

From the Diary of Lemuel Sweet, May 23, 1805

Now, when I most need my liberty, I find it desperately abridged. I am suspected of trifling with the Dutchman's personal effects. Although I am not accused of stealing anything—as indeed I have not—it is true that I have attempted to destroy the bottles he keeps in his quarters. Each is emerald green, about the size of a fist, stopped with a Bulb of a substance I cannot identify. And could not open. I tried every means at my disposal. Nothing would suffice either to open the bottles or to destroy them.

No one understands my motive in attempting to do so, & of course I am not eager to advertise it. Speaking of my suspicions may well earn me a session with the cat—something I do not think I could bear in my present state. I acted only because the situation has become desperate. I know in my heart that the Colonel is behind the death of the Padre Rivera. I suspect his foul work as well in the killing of our interpreter, the pitiable Mr. Scarecrow, and the young girl we met among the Bedouin by the sea, as well as at least three of the juveniles of this town.

These last crimes are blamed on us. The Arabs have come to believe that we drink the blood of their children; that we are evil, & bent on their Destruction. Yet it is not we who do this butchery but one whom we brought with us; & trusted; & allowed to lead us through the Waste. I see now the outlines of his project: Confusion. Fear. And ceaseless bloodshed. And I know too what I must do. I will kill the demon's physical form. I will rend it, piece by piece, into flinders, & I will send each piece separately to the bottom of the ocean. I must do it. And as the time available to me grows short, I must do it now.

Without my friend MacLeish, and with the priest's death, I am sore bereft of allies. I find I have no choice but to enlist the help of my General. He is much beleaguered, but in my Heart I believe him still to be fair and open-minded. I will therefore unfold the matter to him, and pray to the Almighty that He will listen. For if he will not, I fear we are all destined to meet with a violent and untimely end.

25.

Confined to Quarters

Weston holds his hands to his head and rubs his temples. "And tell me again why you were in the Colonel's quarters?"

"It was something he said, sir. About his bottles."

"The bottles."

"The green ones. He said he kept a little girl's…"

"Yes, yes. I know what he said. Or what you think he said. He keeps the soul of a little Berber girl in one of those bottles. Indeed, you claim to have seen her face—or the image of her face—in the glass. And you have a theory as well about the dagger, yes? The one that was found in your friend MacLeish's possession?"

"I do, sir. Or possibly just a suspicion."

"All right, then. Out with it."

"The Colonel."

"Ah. The Colonel again. He put it there?"

"I suspect he wants to turn Private MacLeish against the rest of us. I know it sounds queer."

"Indeed it does. Queer indeed. Why would he want to do that?"

"Because it is his nature. It's all he's *ever* done. For as long as men have been on Earth, the thing that animates Colonel Ladendorf has sought to turn us one against the other. Turk against Christian. Christian against Jew…"

The general sighs. He leans forward and his chair groans beneath him. His eyes are bloodshot, and he needs a shave. He no longer bothers to button his jacket.

"Private Sweet, we are outnumbered here. I trust you can see that. I trust you can see also that we are all that stands in the way of terror and chaos in this city. Ali Rasmin is poised to attack. In fact, I'm surprised he hasn't done so already. Sheikh al-Tahib would rather burn the city and everyone in it than give it back to Rasmin. Meanwhile, the newly liberated citizens of Derna are growing restless. They now celebrate our sacrifices by throwing stones at our patrols. They burn our ridiculous hats—though I would be happy to burn the damn things myself, if asked. Because we are such a small band of compatriots, I have allowed myself considerable latitude with my American brethren during the expedition. I may be at fault for this lenience. In fact, I'm *sure* I'm at fault. But this lenience has given me the chance to study my marines, including you, closely, and I've come to believe you are a promising young man. Presentable. Well-spoken. However—no, let me speak. However, it does you no credit to engage in flights of fancy of this sort. You suffered a shock to your system when you were lost in the desert. I understand that. I still cannot fathom how you could have found yourself in the midst of a massacre of the thieves who took Prince Ahmad's horses and yet have no recollection of the event or its authors. It has also been reported to me that you no longer sleep, and that you have separated yourself from your comrades. That you brood, and seem ill at ease. War will do strange things to a man. I've seen it. I know. But be that as it may, and all extenuating circumstances notwithstanding, I warn you, Private, that another accusation against one of my officers will earn you a flogging before the words have left your mouth. Do you understand me?"

"I do, sir."

"I really hope you do."

"I understand…completely."

"Good. Because I am confining you to quarters. You are privy to information regarding Ambassador Lear's work that cannot be repeated, and you are, at the same time, exhibiting signs of mental instability. I am therefore relieving you of your duties. Mr. Mason? Step inside, please. Mr. Mason will see you to your new billet. The rest of us have work to do, and very little time in which to do it. That is all."

26.

Departure

The evening starts strangely. Sweet has been placed under guard in a small room just inside the city's north wall, so close to the sea that he can hear the sighs of the surf. He wakes from sour dreams to find that his Egyptian minder is absent. Instead, a large man stands in the shadows. There is something familiar about him. The great bulk of the torso; the set of his shoulders. It's Donald MacLeish, barbarous and unshaven, clad in nothing but his jacket and britches and a pair of knee-high black boots. Fine boots. *Officer's boots.* Sweet has trouble believing his eyes. His old friend smiles to see him awaken. He pours Sweet a cup of water from a pitcher beside his bed. The little room is stiflingly hot, and the private drinks gratefully. Greedily. He would drink his own piss at this point. It's not the best water he's ever had, but he takes the pitcher from the marine's hand and drains it.

"I know the truth," says MacLeish.

"The truth?"

The big man nods. "You know what I mean. About the Dutchman. And I'm willing to bear a hand."

"What do you know?"

"Don't doubt me, Sweetie. I know. The priest flapped his red rag to more 'n just you. Ladendorf is of another army altogether, and no friend to the likes of us."

Sweet runs a hand through his hair. He brings back a palm coated with oil and sand. "Thank God. Thank *God.* I wondered if I had lost my senses."

"You had the right of it, my son."

"We need weapons," says Sweet. "And who knows if weapons will work against this monster."

"Steady on," MacLeish answers. He brandishes two pistols. He hands one, butt first, to Sweet. "I'm a step ahead of you. Don't worry. It's charged and primed. I know where to find him. He still fancies you. Get him to talking. Distract him, like. I'll creep up as pretty as you please and put a ball through the back of his skull."

"He's not like us," says Sweet. "He's dangerous. And cunning. Will this really—?"

"Will blowing the back of his head off play arse with his evening? I suspect it will. Whatever his plans for further mischief."

"Padre Rivera said…"

"Padre Rivera was a bloody corpse, last time I checked. Are you willing, or no?"

Sweet takes the pitcher again and gulps down a last few drops. Time is working against them. The sun is disappearing in the west. It is beautiful, he realizes. Scarlet and purple and blue. He could sit and watch awhile. *What would it hurt?* His cot is filthy, but it seems inviting. But no. He shakes his head. *Work to do.* And here is MacLeish—just the man who can help him do it. He feared he'd lost him. His best friend. He rises from the bed to embrace the big man. MacLeish hugs him back.

"It has gone sore for me not to have you with me," says Sweet.

"For me as well."

"You know the risk?"

"There's no risk," growls MacLeish. "I'll tell you where to find the devil. You leave the rest to me. It's going to be a raw red night."

* * *

Sweet meets up with Ladendorf in an alley just east of the *souk*. Even with MacLeish guiding him half the way, it has taken him longer to get here than he wanted. His mind wanders, and the marketplace is dark. Suspecting that the Governor has finally received artillery from Tripoli, Weston has ordered a black-out of the city. In the gloom of dusk, the streets and alleys of Derna seem to have no rational scheme at all. Shadows flit and flicker around him, trembling in the light of Sweet's lantern. Piles of rubble clog the narrow byways, testament to the American bombardment, and the smell of rotting bodies lingers in the evening air.

Colonel Ladendorf is not supposed to know the bad news. The treaty with Tripoli. Admiral Barron's orders. And yet of course he does. He seems untroubled by these developments.

"Congratulate yourself, Private Sweet," he says. "You and your countrymen have brought the blessings of liberty to this pitiful land."

The marine tries to explain. The general has been betrayed. *Diplomats. Tobias Lear. A notorious lickspittle. Some say he poisoned General Washington.*

"But you have *triumphed* here. Shown the sword. Killed scores of men, women, and children. Not to mention the camels and mules. Did you see bodies of the family slain by a ball from *Endeavor*? Cut the mother cleanly in two. The Republic's reputation will grow, yes?"

"I did not see the bodies, but I am aware of the incident. It is regrettable indeed. As is the destruction of the Old Mosque. But that wasn't the point."

"And you, Private Sweet. You killed two men yourself, did you not? That was splendid work. The blade in the guts. Twisting it. An agonizing death. No one thought you could do it. But you can murder just as well as the rest of them, can't you? I suspect your mother will strut and preen when she hears of your exploits."

Sweet struggles to control his temper. "You're not listening. That wasn't the point."

"You came to this country with swords and muskets, not ploughshares. Of course it was the point, you simpering moron. It is *always* the point. You are a butcher and your people are butchers and you wave flags over the corpses so you can tell yourselves you've done something other than simple murder. If Cain had had a flag, he would have planted it in his dead brother's belly and tried to salute it."

"The point was to rescue our countrymen, as you are well aware. But also to restore Prince Ahmad to his rightful seat. And to offer these people a glimpse of the benefits of self-government."

Ladendorf allows himself a crooked smile.

"Ahmad's grandfather won that throne sixty years ago through bloodshed and treachery. There *is* no rightful seat. No king more deserving than another. Is that what you gutted your two Arabs for? So that Ahmad, rather than his brother, could have the privilege of treating his subjects like pack animals?"

Sweet knows better than to argue.

"It will be dangerous for you here, Colonel."

"I know. All the Christians are to be taken off. Except for the priest, I suppose."

"Not Padre Rivera. You took care of that."

Ladendorf whispers, as if sharing a secret. "And a bloody bag of guts he *was*, too. But he enjoyed it. All priests enjoy dying for the faith. Martyred for the sake of their dirty little rabbi. He is with his Brotherhood at last. The largest of the Brotherhoods, that vast and plaintive union of the dead. Little cesspools for the worms to explore. But he did share a story with me before he passed. Something about a ring, and an angel, and a Hebrew king named Solomon. Yes? You thought I didn't know? You thought the priest would be able to keep a secret from me as I pulled his eyes from his head? Don't worry, Private Sweet. I won't join the general in his disgraceful evacuation. Someday I'll see this wondrous country of yours—this nation of virtues surpassing all others. But I still have work to do in Tripoli. And then, who knows? I suspect I shall have to see just how powerful the ring really is. There are stories, you know."

"What work?"

Ladendorf looks at him blankly.

P.t. Donald MacLeish

"You said you had work to do. In Tripoli."

"Ah. Yes. Killing Yusuf Vartoonian."

"Why do you care about King Yusuf, if his claim is no worse than his brother's?"

"Yusuf has imprisoned my daughter. He keeps her in a cage. From time to time she is called upon to advise the king on matters beyond his understanding."

"She's the witch. In the Red Palace."

"She is not a *witch*. Yusuf wished for a prize. She gave him a fine American warship, stuck on Kaliusa like a whale washed ashore on the beach. He was supposed to free her then. But he broke his promise. And now his treasure has turned to ashes in his grasp."

"I had no idea. You must be disappointed in…what has happened."

"I will see her free again. I always do."

"And King Yusuf?"

"I will peel the skin from his head and feed it to his children."

No humor now. The colonel's thin lips are pinched tight with malice. And so they stand looking at each other. Sweet feels a bead of sweat run down his back.

"You find my presence troubling."

"I don't understand," says Sweet.

"You do understand. Your pistol is charged."

The young marine is no longer so easily embarrassed.

"There was a letter to the general. It said you were lost. Or that…Colonel *Ladendorf* was lost. Presumed dead."

"What's wrong?"

"Nothing is wrong."

"You're sleepy. Did you drink the water I sent you?"

"You?"

"Yes. Earlier today. By your bed. With a little something extra."

"I thought…Donald."

"Ah. Private MacLeish. My very good friend. You're quite right. It was he who actually brought it to you."

"You're dead. *Presumed* dead. In 1735."

"I added a little sherry," says Ladendorf. "Some saffron. And the laudanum, of course. The priest's little friend. Things must look queer to you just about now."

"Many years ago."

"Many years ago…? Yes? I'm listening. Speak your mind." The colonel grins. His big tongue probes the corners of his mouth like a curious snake. His breath is the breeze from a slaughterhouse.

"Presumed dead. *You* were…presumed dead. Many years ago."

"That is a problem."

Sweet's eyes widen. "If you're dead, how can I kill you?"

"How indeed?" Ladendorf looks back over Sweet's shoulder and nods. "It makes the head dizzy."

The big man can move quietly when he wants to. Donald MacLeish steps out of the darkness and splits the back of Sweet's skull open with the butt of his pistol. Sweet twists, staggers, goes to his knees. He looks up to see who has attacked him and finds it is worse than he imagined. He notices the ruby ring on a finger of MacLeish's right hand. He has to warn his friend, but his mouth is unable to make the words.

No, he says. Or tries to say. *Please.*

MacLeish chuckles. He places a boot on Sweet's chest and gives him a shove. The young man falls hard.

"Thought you'd take my place, eh Sweetie? Wanted the ring?"

"No," says Sweet. It's the most he can manage. He wants to say it a hundred times. *No No No No No No.*

"Take off the Joseph's coat, you little shit. You ain't gettin' the gold, and you ain't going with us."

"Don't take him," says Sweet. He speaks directly to Ladendorf. The sound is more croak than command.

"Him?" says the Dutchman. He squats beside Sweet. He is clearly enjoying the conversation.

"MacLeish. He's not all bad. He's my friend."

"Of course he's not all bad. He's a splendid, strapping fellow. He can crush a man's windpipe in the time it takes you to swat a fly."

"He has a child back home. A son."

"Pity."

"Don't. Take *me* if you have to. I'm asking you as civil as I know how."

Ladendorf sighs. "And I'm telling you, Private Sweet, that it doesn't matter what you ask. Donald?"

MacLeish gives the young man a kick to the side of the head.

Ladendorf stands. "Splendid. That will do for now. You're quite ready, Private MacLeish?"

"Ready as I'll ever be."

"You're reporting for duty?"

"I'm—"

MacLeish flinches from the colonel's touch, and for a moment doubt flickers on his face like light from a dying candle. But a moment is all he gets. Ladendorf grabs MacLeish's right wrist with his left hand. The Dutchman forms a trowel with the fingers of his other hand and shoves it into the big man's stomach. Sweet hears the wet thick sound of tearing flesh. MacLeish's scream echoes off the stone walls. A dog barks in the next street over, and somewhere nearby two doors slam shut in quick succession.

In his state of semi-consciousness Sweet sees Ladendorf working his forearms up into MacLeish's torso. MacLeish emits vague tortured squeals and his eyes go wide with shock as the Dutchman thrusts his head into the big man's open abdomen as if to gaze behind the curtain of tissue and gristle at some particularly compelling theatrical performance. There is an interlude of silence, and then a hiss of escaping air. As the Dutchman's body goes limp, a figure charred black as if badly burned but glistening with viscous internal gelatins like a stillborn calf encased in its caul wriggles up out of the sagging corpse and into its new host in a mad parodical inversion of natural birth. The thing is larval and long-fingered and so dark that it seems to drain light from the night around it; indeed, looking at it is like gazing into a demented mirror in which one's image is not cast back but rather sucked *in*, and *through*, toward dismal and unholy worlds beyond. Sweet's senses revolt at the pageant of this bizarre infestation: at the agony etched on MacLeish's face and the trembling in his knees and the soft sticky rumors of the big man's organs being displaced and rearranged. The young marine's heart throbs in his chest. The veins in his temples are tight with blood and it is impossible to tell if the figure worming its way into MacLeish is large or small, fully formed or wholly inchoate. Hard to say also if the process takes a minute or an hour. Sweet's pulse accelerates and time seems to slow down, to rest upon him like a fallen city.

Ladendorf's vacant form slowly collapses like one of the goats the young private has watched the Bedouin butcher. The goat rarely struggles. More bewildered than angry, it simply sinks to earth as the life force spills from its open throat. MacLeish stands silent, save for the blood dripping from his belly onto the paving stones with an irregular patter like the run-off from a fitful rain. All is still in the district around them. From far off comes the Mahometan call to prayer. It is the night prayer, the *Isha*, performed when the final red thread has disappeared from the western sky. Sweet thinks, *How can anyone pray on an evening like this?* But of course this night is no different than any other, and the words rise like mist on a mountain lake.

✹ ✹ ✹

MacLeish opens his eyes. They are yellow now, like the dead Dutchman's. The big man stares down at Sweet without seeming to recognize him. A moment later, a grin spreads his face. He flexes his hands, straightens his spine with an audible pop. He steps over the mess of meat and skin that was Colonel Ladendorf and kneels beside the injured marine. Sweet tries to see through the blood in his eyes. *Funny how the night has turned to liquid,* he thinks. *Queer how the sky flows past. Like a river. Like…*

"Don't do it," he says. His voice is little more than a gasp.

"It's done," says MacLeish. The *new* MacLeish. "Lie still. I just need a few things from you, my boy. Some savory things. To keep us strong, MacLeish and I. And then…your head."

"My head."

The big man nods. "You see, Private Sweet, we've joined the other side. *Turned Turk,* I think you say. We shall bring your pretty head to the Governor to prove we wish to join King Yusuf's army, and I, Donald MacLeish, of the United States Marines, will promise Yusuf intelligence of General Weston's treacherous intentions to break the new treaty. To gain an audience, you see? And then I'll kill the sniveling son of a whore. Listen. Do you hear the muskets? I sent word to the Governor earlier this evening that the Christians are running away. Derna is his for the taking. His scouts are entering the city. If your friends haven't escaped to the ships already, they'll be stone dead by sunrise."

To Sweet the world has lost all meaning. What was Ladendorf is now MacLeish, and what was MacLeish is something repellent: a rutted, blistered face with yellow eyes and yawning black nostrils. A face like hell. Hell opened up.

The djinn. *A demon.*

"One day I'll see your new country," it whispers.

Flat on his back, Sweet tries to inch away. He tightens the muscles of his shoulders, hoping to move. He fails. MacLeish takes one of his hands in his own.

"And I'll be sure to visit your sister."

Without even blinking, the thing snaps Sweet's left ring finger. The young man cries out before he quite knows what has happened. MacLeish chuckles. He stoops to lick Sweet's throat. He opens his mouth, and his teeth are long and jagged and clotted with flesh. He bends so close that Sweet can feel the hot breath on his skin, and now his voice is the voice of the slaughtered priest, intimate and mocking. "Goodbye, Private Sweet. *Vaya con Dios.*"

And then the creature lunges to its feet.

In the shadows around them stand a dozen figures. They have arrived without sound—almost as if they were present all along, but waiting to make their presence known. The largest of the figures holds an immense sword, jeweled at the hilt, glinting like dawn. The rest carry halberds, maces, battle axes. Each has words in Latin tattooed in blue ink across his forehead. *Punishment. Absolution. Redemption.* They are bearded, cold-eyed men, clad in iron and as grim as death. Together they form a rough circle around the spot where Sweet lies.

"Hold, worm," says the sword bearer. The cross of St. George is emblazoned on his tunic. He holds the broadsword with both hands. "You have something that belongs to another."

"Impossible," hisses MacLeish. Because the demon is MacLeish again. Sweet can see clearly. Perhaps it is the opium speaking—he knows this—but it seems to him that for the first time in his life he can peer beneath appearances into the truth of things and see at last the grand archaic battles beside him of piety and darkness, angel and demon, the sharp acidic forces of mayhem and chaos beating hard against the fortress of faith. The unclean thing crouching over him is MacLeish and it is not—MacLeish in *seeming*;

something ugly and unknowable within. And gazing out at the world with those vicious little crow eyes.

The night sky beyond the demon eddies and swirls. Stars dance in place. Somehow hours have passed; the constellations have all wheeled west. The walls of the alley tower over the fallen marine like cliffs.

"You are a *thief*," says the sword bearer. "You are a thief and an abomination. Give us the ring, or by God's strength we will take it from you."

And there it is, on MacLeish's right hand. MacLeish glances down at the gold band. Sweet cannot blame him. Even betrayed by the man, he still cares for his great true troubled friend—or what is left of his friend. Whether it is the Seal of Solomon or not, the ring is an object of great promise and power, and truly beautiful.

The thing that is MacLeish turns to assess the forces arrayed against it. It bolts, is intercepted, is shoved back into the center of the circle. The demon speaks now in some guttural tongue that seems composed in equal parts of filth and fury; indeed it is not spoken so much as *spat* at the figures in attendance, a torrent of abuse that fouls the very air in which it moves. The knights edge closer nevertheless, weapons raised, poised to strike. MacLeish seizes Sweet and holds him like a shield. The demon's hands are so strong, the pain so fierce, that the young marine is roused from his stupor. Realizing he is about to be cut to pieces, he does the only thing he can. He pulls the pistol from his sash. He holds it to his best friend's head and he fires.

* * *

Sweet sees little of what happens next. He is dropped, or thrown, and he hits the ground hard. The knights hack and thrust at the demon as it hurls curses in its ugly cellar shriek. The creature stumbles as it struggles with the men around it. Two of them fall, but a half-dozen of the figures force the big marine to his knees. A hammer connects with the back of MacLeish's neck with a dull thud. Several of the knights ride their foe, face-down, into the dust of the alley and wrestle the creature's right arm out in front of it. One man drops to his knees and holds a crucifix inches from the demon's eyes. He speaks in Latin. Sweet recognizes the words, and joins in their recital.

In nomine Patris, et Filii, et Spiritus Sancti...

"I can't be *killed, you fools!*" says the demon. It looks less like Sweet's friend now. Its skin is crawling—*decaying,* as if eaten by some unseen flame. It spits and screams and the air grows thick with the odor of putrefaction. Blood seeps from its eyes and mouth. It thrashes and bucks in the dirt, trying desperately to break the hold of its captors, until at last one of the knights drives his lance through the thing's lower back and thereby pins it in place.

"So it is written," says the figure with the sword. He alone has stood unmoving during the struggle. He steps forward, studying the writhing figure in front of him as if it were some loathsome species of insect. Then he raises the blade. "We who sinned against the Almighty have been brought forth from the dust to chastise the sins of others. You are a liar and a thief. You have murdered the Father's children and dragged them into confusion and darkness. You cannot be *killed,* worm. But you can be punished."

The sword bearer brings the blade down. It slices through flesh and bone and sparks fly when it hits stone beneath the body. The demon's howl splits the night like a knife. MacLeish's severed fingers land just a few inches from Sweet's face, still twitching with nervous energy. The man with the sword stoops to pick up one of the digits. He removes the ring from the flesh and places the object in a pouch he wears at his waist. The finger is tossed aside.

The sword bearer cocks his head. Someone is coming.

Two figures.

Soldiers.

"Bring the creature," says the man to his followers.

With these words, the crusaders disappear from Sweet's sight like the tail of some dark star falling fast across the troubled face of midnight, bearing with them the struggling form of Donald MacLeish.

* * *

In the early morning hours Malcolm Weston, his staff, and the Christian soldiers are retrieved by longboats from *Endeavor*. Ahmad Vartoonian comes too, with ten of his followers. General Weston is so despondent that he declines to enforce his orders against looting the city. The Greeks therefore clamber aboard with sacks full of valuables: silverware and candlesticks, daggers and damask and purple silk. They have also found or made a quantity of date wine, and, once on the ship, set about consuming it with vigor. The Egyptians and Prince Ahmad's men are silent and deathly still. There is no color in their faces.

The marines linger on shore, as their lieutenant has volunteered them to hold the beach until everyone else is safely away. But there is considerable confusion. Colonel Ladendorf and Privates Sweet and MacLeish are nowhere to be found. Corrigan refuses to depart without his men. He holds no great affection for either Ladendorf or MacLeish, but this is beside the point. The lieutenant has elevated ideas about the practice of warfare. Among them is the notion that a marine should never leave a man behind. Captain Burrus of *Endeavor* is less starry-eyed. He has a note rowed in to the beach, demanding to know the cause of the delay. Cursing, the lieutenant dispatches Stennett and Prejean to find their missing comrades. Sweet was last seen near the Governor's palace, moving slowly, with a blank look in his eyes. The marines hustle toward the center of the city. They hear a pistol shot, and stop at one end of a dirty alley near the market. From a distance it appears that a number of people have gathered around a fallen body. There is indistinct but violent movement, a confusion of shadows. They both hear the scream. It is so ferocious that they almost turn back. They stand for several moments until their hearts slow and their sense of duty returns. When the marines finally move forward, the figures have disappeared.

Lemuel Sweet lies face-up in a puddle of his own blood. A few feet away, a dog is sniffing a small dark object that turns out to be, on further inspection, a human heart. Stennett chases the cur with a boot to the belly. Beside Sweet are three severed fingers and what appears to be a corpse—possibly that of Colonel Ladendorf. It is not really a body but rather a *hide*, a shell of a carcass emptied of form and fluid. The two marines try to peel it out of the puddle, but it rips in their hands. The stench of death rises like a fog from the mess. Prejean excuses himself, and Stennett hears the little marine vomiting a few feet away.

When he returns, Prejean rouses Sweet by pouring water from his goatskin over his head. It takes several moments for the younger man to recall his companions' faces. The Marines hoist Sweet to his feet. There is no time for the usual courtesies. They need to move quickly. Sheikh al-Tahib's followers are suspicious, they report. They sense betrayal, and the way to the beach may already be blocked.

Prejean suggests one final street to check in the search for MacLeish, but Sweet knows better. MacLeish is somewhere with the Dutchman. MacLeish *is* the Dutchman. Or the other way around. Or something in between. MacLeish is in the cold company of the dead, and he will not soon be found.

Sweet tries to focus. "Leave now," he says.

The three men stumble from city to shore in the brown light of dawn like mummers in some pantomime of drunken regret, Sweet supported between his rescuers like a reluctant bridegroom but smeared with blood from head to toe. He suspects he is dying. He has trouble moving his feet.

Corrigan sees them reach the strand and damns them with every breath. A half-dozen Arabs spill out of the shadows behind them, daggers and scimitars drawn. A hundred yards away, Repentance Moore looks down along the barrel of his Dickert rifle with one cold gray eye. A shot rings out, and an Arab falls. A sailor hands Moore a loaded musket and he sights and fires again. Corrigan draws his saber, but the Arabs break off their pursuit. Sweet is hauled into the longboat as Moore, Prejean, and Stennett shove the vessel into the surf and belly up into it. Musket balls whine overhead, but none finds its mark.

"MacLeish?" asks Corrigan. "The Colonel?"

"Gone, sir."

"What do you mean, *gone?* Are they dead?"

Stennett turns to Sweet. Sweet nods. "Dead," he says.

Or worse. This thought goes unspoken.

Endeavor's foresail luffs in the morning breeze. The sun comes up, and Sheikh al-Tahib and a dozen of his tribesmen watch from the shore as the American ships prepare to depart. The Arabs scream and point, but only the faintest sounds reach the marines. Words of reproach and damnation. Scattered musket fire. Within an hour, the governor's cavalry appears on the beach. The marines see fighting. Tiny figures. The antic pageant of statecraft, mounted for the amusement of any who care to watch. Soon the scarlet flag of King Yusuf rises over the governor's palace. Of al-Tahib's ninety horsemen, fourteen escape into the desert. The sheikh himself is ridden down, pierced by a dozen blades, and unceremoniously beheaded. Derna is no longer a bastion of liberty. Derna is a slaughterhouse.

The frigate's sails fill their bellies with wind. Weston and his men are off to Malta. For America, the war is over. Sweet wants to tell the citizens of Derna. He is not sure they know. But first an errand. He has words to say to the architect of all madness and beauty. He came to this country with noble ambitions and has fled under cover of darkness, wishing in part to be dead. If he lives, he will no longer dwell in the pages of natural history. There is nothing natural about what he has seen. He will study the human story instead, and write of horror and hatred and all the red red blood that stains his hands. *Can a nation kill with honor?* he wonders. *Can a man do murder justly or at all and bear to hear a loved one call his name? Can truths that are self-evident to a people on one side of an ocean seem repellent to a province on the other?*

It is done. The breeze stiffens. Africa sinks below the horizon.

"God," the private whispers. "Forgive us."

The End

37388189R00106

Made in the USA
San Bernardino, CA
16 August 2016